REMNANTS

REMNANTS

CÉLINE HUYGHEBAERT

TRANSLATED BY ALESHIA JENSEN

Book*hug Press
Toronto 2022

Literature in Translation Series

FIRST ENGLISH EDITION

Published originally under the title *Le drap blanc* © Céline Huyghebaert
and Le Quartanier, Montreal, 2019

English translation © 2022 by Aleshia Jensen

Library and Archives Canada Cataloguing in Publication

Title: Remnants / Céline Huyghebaert ; translated by Aleshia Jensen.
Other titles: Drap blanc. English
Names: Huyghebaert, Céline, author. | Jensen, Aleshia, translator.
Series: Literature in translation series.
Description: Series statement: Literature in translation series |
Translation of: Le drap blanc.
Identifiers: Canadiana (print) 20210376295 | Canadiana (ebook) 20210376309
ISBN 9781771667500 (softcover)
ISBN 9781771667517 (EPUB)
ISBN 9781771667524 (PDF)
Classification: LCC PS8615.U94 D7313 2022 | DDC C842/.6—dc23

The production of this book was made possible through the generous assistance
of the Canada Council for the Arts and the Ontario Arts Council.
Book*hug Press also acknowledges the support of the Government of Canada through
the Canada Book Fund and the Government of Ontario through
the Ontario Book Publishing Tax Credit and the Ontario Book Fund.

Book*hug Press acknowledges that the land on which we operate
is the traditional territory of many nations, including the Mississaugas
of the Credit, the Anishnabeg, the Chippewa, the Haudenosaunee,
and the Wendat peoples. We recognize the enduring presence of many
diverse First Nations, Inuit, and Métis peoples and are grateful
for the opportunity to meet, work, and learn on this territory.

And I told myself I would forget when he was there, in the white room. I would forget it all. His hands beneath the sheet…

—Laurent Mauvignier, *Apprendre à finir*

REMNANTS

REMNANTS

DIALOGUES

PRELUDE

CÉLINE: François?

FRANÇOIS: Yes?

CÉLINE: It's Céline Huyghebaert... How are you?

FRANÇOIS: Good, good. *(They both laugh uneasily.)* Yourself?

CÉLINE: It's been a long time...

FRANÇOIS: Yes. A long time...

CÉLINE: Is Jeanne there? Can I talk to her?

FRANÇOIS: Of course.

The sound of the receiver placed on the table, muffled voices, crackling.

JEANNE: Hello?

The first thing Céline hears is how much her aunt's voice is like her father's—stony. Then Jeanne says "Hello?" again and Céline also hears a "No," a categorical refusal that should make her hang up straight away.

CÉLINE: It's Céline. How are you?

JEANNE: I'm well.

CÉLINE: I'm glad I was able to reach you. I left a few messages, but you never returned my calls.

JEANNE: We're only here six months a year now, you know.

CÉLINE: You've got a house somewhere?

JEANNE: No, just a plot of land with a bungalow. We come back to Plaisir for the winter.

CÉLINE: Ah, okay.

JEANNE: And yourself?

CÉLINE: I'm still living in Quebec. I like it. I'm going to school. But I'm in France for a few weeks. It'd be nice to see you while I'm here.

JEANNE: Why's that?

CÉLINE: I'm doing research for a book I'm writing about Papa. I wanted to talk to you about it. And find out how you've been. We haven't seen each other since Papa died.

JEANNE: Well, there's not much I can tell you about him.

CÉLINE: I wanted to know more about when the two of you were growing up, what things were like before I was born.

JEANNE: I raised him like a son, and I can't even remember anything about my own sons, so there's really not much I can tell you about your father.

CÉLINE: Maybe if we saw each other in person, a few stories would—

JEANNE: No. No...

CÉLINE: Maybe you could lend me your photo albums so I can scan some pictures of him?

JEANNE: No, that's not possible.

CÉLINE: It's not just for my project. It's for us: his daughters. So we can have something to remember him by.

JEANNE: You've already got pictures of him.

CÉLINE: Not from when he was little.

JEANNE: There aren't very many from back then. We didn't have a camera, you know.

CÉLINE: Even if there are just a few...

JEANNE: I'd have to look around for them. They're buried somewhere. It's not something I can find just like that.

CÉLINE: That's no problem. I could come by this weekend if you like.

JEANNE: Right, well, I'll think about it.

CÉLINE: I could even help you look for them.

JEANNE: I don't know.

Extended pause.

CÉLINE: I'm guessing that if I give you my number, you won't call me back?

JEANNE: No.

CÉLINE: So maybe I could call you sometime before Friday? Would that give you some time?

JEANNE: *(Firmly)* No—no. I'd rather you didn't.

CÉLINE: You don't want me to come by?

JEANNE: All that's in the past. Buried. I'll be joining him soon, in any case.

CÉLINE: I don't understand. I'm just asking to look at the pictures, that's all.

JEANNE: I've lost a daughter and two sons. I've lost my three brothers. I don't want to think about that anymore.

CÉLINE: But—

JEANNE: I lost my brother. What do you want me to say? I don't live in the past. There's no point.

CÉLINE: That's not it, I don't want to live in the past, but—

JEANNE: I'm sorry but I have to hang up.

CÉLINE: All right.

Long silence. Céline stays quiet, hoping the awkward pause might make Jeanne give in. But Jeanne doesn't say anything.

CÉLINE: I hope you get everything you deserve in life.

There's audible frustration in her voice.

JEANNE: *(Unexpectedly tender)* You too. And your sisters. I wish all of you the best. Goodbye.

Long silence.

CÉLINE: *(Gently)* Bye.

Then the call ends. The silences and failures to understand still intact on both ends of the line.

Jeanne dies of a pulmonary embolism six years later.

MAGRITTE'S FACE

/ 1

I've never told Martin how much he looks like my father. That's what
I'm thinking as the food arrives at the table and Martin tells me about
his week in detailed chronological order. I murmur *mm-hmm* a few too
many times, like a journalist feigning enthusiasm during an interview.

"How's the meat—good? More wine?"

Instead of answering, I scan Martin's face for traces of my father.
He has the same thin lips hidden under a thick beard and, when he
smiles, the same tooth missing on top, a black hole he promises to get
filled as soon as he has the money—fine, but when will that be?—which
he probes with the tip of his tongue as if expecting something to have
suddenly sprouted there.

We're at Thursday evening now. I would cut in and change the
subject, but the thing is, I'm looking for a reason to start a fight. He's
telling me about a movie he went to by himself. Just hearing the title
makes me vaguely listless.

"The first few seconds of any movie are crucial, right? So the first
thing we see is a still frame of a goldfish in a tank. Remember that,
it's important. Then pan to Gabita's hands, and her legs—she's waxing
them—then a wide shot with her roommate, Otilia."

Martin picks up the water pitcher and fills our glasses. Now he's going to explain the movie scene by scene, even though he knows how utterly tedious I find this.

"We're in Romania, just before the fall of Ceaușescu. I know what you're thinking. I get too wrapped up in the details, but I'm telling you because you need to know if you want to understand Gabita's situation: she's a few months pregnant, in a country where abortion is illegal."

My ears perk up a bit.

"There's this scene near the end, Otilia is with her boyfriend in the bedroom. They're sitting across from each other, knees almost touching. It would almost be sensual, except Otilia's just admitted that she helped Gabita get an abortion. 'That's what the money was for?' her boyfriend asks. And Otilia looks up, clearly very angry. She could tell him everything she and Gabita had gone through, but instead she answers, 'Is that how much you think an abortion costs: three hundred lei?'"

I take the saltshaker from Martin's hand.

"Then she asks him, 'And what would you do if I got pregnant?' He answers, 'Don't start. That would never happen.' 'Oh yeah? Wouldn't it?' she says. 'So you've already thought about it?' She's speaking softly but you can tell she's angry. Her eyes say it all."

It's hard to tell where Otilia's irritation ends and mine begins.

"But she keeps going. 'How can you be so sure it won't happen? It's not like you know when I get my period.' And then, get this, he says, 'If you got pregnant, I'd ask you to marry me.'"

I look at Martin, furious.

"I think that's the exact moment she goes from being angry to being sad, because she realizes she's exactly like the goldfish swimming in circles in the fishbowl in her room. She's stuck."

"What about you?"

Martin looks at me, surprised, and smiles. "What about me?"

"What would you do if I was pregnant?"

He takes his pocket knife, opens it and rests it on the table, pushing the restaurant knife aside. He seems wary, and suddenly very quiet. He looks straight at me. He can tell I'm prodding at him, and skirts the question I've laid out like a trap.

"More wine?"

"Not your fucking problem, right?"

"Right, that's it. Not my fucking problem," he says.

"You wouldn't have said that before."

He cuts into his ribeye, stabs a big piece with his fork, and then a few fries, dips the whole thing in mayonnaise and lowers his head to the height of the wineglasses, opening his mouth wide to stuff the whole thing in. He chews slowly, swallows and exhales. "Before what, Céline?"

That's my cue. Martin's answer is a pretext, but it could easily have been the knife splayed open on the table, the same kind my father used to open and lay next to his plate every night at dinner. Or Martin's lean physique, so like the one my mother didn't dare leave for over twenty long years, my mother who aged before her time, never feeling loved other than as a mother. I look at Martin and my anger swells as I think of a future where I'm the mother of his children, who are frail like him, with thin lips and weak teeth, children without a hope of doing better than us. And yet we'll still have them when the time comes. That Martin doesn't see what looms over these hypothetical lives angers me the most.

And now I'm not sure anymore whether I'm mad at him for his lack of character or for what a sad man my father was. I tell him he's always hiding behind his armour, and I feel sorry for him. I know deep down I've started this pathetic argument because my love for Martin, the first man in my life as a girl without a father, unsettles me.

/ 2

On the way home, I ended up explaining to Martin why I was in such a bad mood. I hoped he'd be able to understand despite me stomping off toward his apartment, stopping mid-sentence to catch my breath. Martin was struggling to keep up; he'd eaten too much. First I told him he couldn't come to my place because a colony of bookworms had invaded my shelves. They were at that very moment devouring the notebooks I'd kept since I'd moved to Montreal. They'd already obliterated five years of memories, boring through from cover to cover, leaving holes like the ones I imagined on the face of the man with the bowler hat. Martin seemed lost, so I started over. One day, I told him, I'd sent my father a greeting card with a picture of Magritte's painting *Man in a Bowler Hat* on the front, and inside I'd written a long message about resilience. Or giving up. Or how close he was to ruining his life for good. Back then I wielded words like bombs, and I'd wanted him to feel my words blow up in his face when he opened the card. But it was such a shock that my father ended up in the hospital. My sister called me, and I had to take the first plane out. In the short time it took me to buckle my seat belt, unbuckle it, cross the Atlantic, rebuckle my seat belt, touch down at Roissy and find my bags on the carousel, my phone rang again. It was my sister. I was too late. He was dead. But don't worry, she added, he knew you loved him.

If Magritte had painted *Man in a Bowler Hat* before the dove flew by, I said to Martin, I think there'd be a hole instead of a face, a big black hole without a nose, mouth or eyes. It wasn't my fault my father had died, Martin answered. He always cut down my emotions at the root, I shot back, but really I wanted Martin to say that again with his arms around me.

"I'm sorry," he said softly.

"It doesn't change anything."

"Would it be better if I went home alone?"

I tried to articulate a thought still too hazy to put into words. It had been on my mind since the evening Martin and I first met, and saying it wouldn't have meant the end of the world. I shrugged. "I don't know."

He smiled. He stopped, slipped a hand into his jacket and pulled out the half-finished bottle of wine from dinner and held it out. It was a Languedoc, an aggressive front of Syrah untampered by the other grapes. The sommelier had talked it up so much that when I first tasted it, all I could do was let out a small sound, which he mistook for enthusiasm.

"Happy anniversary."

Last night had been our fifth anniversary. Right.

/ 3

This morning, I woke up in a rocking chair in the living room, my feet frozen and my neck stiff. Shit. After Martin went home last night, I came back to my place, determined to get rid of the worms once and for all. I put on some music, poured a glass of wine and sorted through all my books and journals, tossing the ones the worms had ruined into a big plastic bag. I tied it up tightly and brought it down to the basement.

When I came back upstairs, the wine hit me, and I figured I shouldn't lie down just yet. So I dealt with the books the worms had spared. One by one I shook them out and wiped the covers with a cloth dampened with pine oil. I poured the oil directly onto the shelves and rubbed every square inch of wood before replacing the books—alphabetically by author, which I'd been meaning to do for a while. Then I moved on to the other wood furniture: the little IKEA side table, the wooden trunk thrifted at Renaissance and the rocking chair, the first and last piece of furniture from my woodworking career, which had lasted all of three months, between my illusions of a making a living by drawing and a sudden passion for organic farming—a small sample of the many hobbies I'd tried in the hopes that my father would notice, even after his death. When I was done, I dropped the cloth next to the rocking chair and sat down, satisfied.

Now, since I got up, I've been staring at the empty space on my bookshelf where my notebooks used to be, between the rumblings of Céline—the writer, not the singer—and Cendrars's peregrinations. The infestation is hard to accept. Five years erased, just like that: the complete transcription of my state of mind since I met Martin, memories of my father meticulously jotted down as they surfaced and even a few observations from the year before his death—not quite sentences, just sequences of words capturing a few seconds of a conversation or disagreement, or the details of a dinner at his place, and anecdotes, but essential ones, because they were written by a girl with a living father, a different girl, with different dreams, a girl unafraid of dying.

I had the pencil drawings I did at the morgue too, the surgically precise notes documenting the chromatic variations of my father's skin, centimetre by centimetre. It's like losing him all over again, not only him but my memories of his death, which was all I had left of him.

The erasure has left me feeling weightless, as painfully light as the day my sisters and I scattered his ashes in the water. There was no celebration. No ceremony. No moment of remembrance. I sank my hands into the box and threw the ashes, even as the wind kept whipping them back toward us. I sneezed, rubbed my eyes, took out another handful of dust and tried to remind myself that this was a body, it had been a body. I was hanging on to the urn's handles, to fistfuls of ashes: it was absurd. It would have taken the weight of a massive tombstone to anchor me to the real world. The first strong wind could have swept me away.

I get up from the rocking chair and pick up the empty bottle, childhood memories wafting up and swirling in my nostrils. I go to the kitchen, throw the bottle into the recycling. I tell myself I could maybe let go of the rest of my memories too, along with my morbid fondness for black holes in books and memories, for the things that bind me to my father's absence. I feel a little better, as though the day has settled back onto a horizontal plane. I empty the garbage and balance the full bag on the recycling bin to save myself another trip down the three storeys of my building.

I step into the sticky heat of a summer come early, but I don't linger on the feeling of it on my face, or on the posters of Magritte I see plastered on the telephone poles at the end of my street. Magritte has gone mainstream. Museums no longer venture retrospectives of his work, and Depardon's catalogue has replaced it as the coffee-table book of choice.

My father had three pipes. Each of his three daughters inherited one. Years after his death, mine still smelled of tobacco, the scent soaking into any nearby object, so that I had the constant impression he was in the room with me. I sealed the pipe in a bag and hid it, and now I don't know where I put it. With any luck, it's in the basement, buried under boxes, perhaps even under notebooks, where it is delicately perfuming the pages with the smell of tobacco, lending fuller form to my father's story.

/ 4

I'd like to write a book about my father. For ages now I've been writing down anything that makes me think of him: quotes, conversations, memories. There's even a notebook for dreams he's in. One day I had an idea to write a novel about him, as a long list of anecdotes. On a page of the notebook, I began writing:

I
He reprimands her for forgetting the coarse salt in the water for the eggs. She's annoyed. "Of course I put the salt in." He's skeptical. "When you cook the eggs with coarse salt, the shells peel off easily." "Do it yourself next time then." This conversation happens often, in this precise order, with these precise words.

II

She sets two bowls on the kitchen table for coffee. Next to them, the sugar. The coffee on the stove is ready. He pours it into his bowl, then adds a splash of cold water to lengthen it. He says, "I don't know how you can drink your coffee boiling hot like that." She takes small, regular sips. The liquid goes down her throat with a loud swallow.

After, he goes to the toilet for a smoke, then washes up and leaves for work. At the table, they always sit side by side, not facing one another.

III

When he gets home from work, the first thing he asks is what's for dinner. As for her, as soon as she's in the door and has taken off her shoes, she goes to their room to change into soft, comfortable clothes.

IIII

In the evening he also says, "I'm tired." And she answers, "Me too. Exhausted. I haven't stopped running all day." He pokes fun: "As if you were working." He tries to get us in on the game: "She's always in the break room drinking coffee." He says he's the one who's dead tired, because he works outside, in the cold, alone. She cries. This happens every week, on as many evenings as there are workdays.

~~IIII~~

Every year for her birthday, Mother's Day and Christmas, she receives dishes from a stoneware set she hopes to have finished collecting by the time the artisan stops producing it. There is a tacit understanding of this ritual's hierarchy. The youngest daughter has the privilege of offering a surprise of her choosing—small objects that are cute but non-essential: salt and pepper shakers, an egg cup, a creamer, a candle holder. The two others add to the small and large plates and everything else that comes in a series, because somebody has to do it. The husband helps the girls finish the set as fast as possible so it can finally be used for special occasions. As for the father-in-law, he comes in strong with the biggest pieces and the soup and salad bowls, which he hopes are expensive enough to make up for the blunders and cutting remarks she's endured from him.

̶H̶H̶ I

They are invited to visit friends. She lays out the clothes she'd like him to wear. She places the clean, ironed pair of jeans on the bed, a T-shirt that doesn't have a logo for a brand of tools or a tractor company. As he does every time, he pretends to refuse to make the slightest effort, puts on his used, comfortable work clothes and struts into the living room like that just to piss her off. Then he changes. On the rarest of occasions, she gambles on a dress shirt and pleated pants, and after lengthy verbal jousting he yields but brings a pair of jeans, a T-shirt and running shoes in a bag, like a woman in heels who plans on dancing later in the evening.

̶H̶H̶ II

Weekends are spent on tasks that can't be finished during the week. Cleaning, shopping, repairs, renovations, painting, cutting wood, caring for the garden. One year, they win an award for their flowers.

̶H̶H̶ III

All she asks is that he turn his socks right-side out and empty his pockets before he puts them in the wash, so random things don't get stuck in the washer drum. It's impossible to know if he even tries to remember. In any case, he's the one who fixes the machine.

I managed to keep writing these until I got to twelve.

̶H̶H̶ ̶H̶H̶ II

He goes to the train station to pick up his father. "Don't spend too long at the café," she tells him, "lunch will be ready at noon." She's waiting for something that should have come with marriage, at least on weekends.

And then that was all I could find, so I put my list of insignificant moments back onto the shelf.

I once asked my mother if she loved my father, and she didn't answer. But later she said, "I was insecure. I needed someone to take an interest in me." And she confided, "He never told me he loved me." "Never?" "Never." I felt undeserving of hearing things so close to her heart. "But you knew he loved you. Even though he didn't say it?" I asked, trying to make it disappear. And she said, "Yes." Yes, of course she knew—but you need to hear it. I hope Martin and I never forget to tell each other what we need to hear, so what we call our love for one another doesn't change into something else: a couple, for instance.

The last few times Martin and I made love, I tried to keep my eyes open, to stay in the moment. The kisses on my forehead, the feel of his skin under my fingers, the cold, the warmth, the inside of my thighs against his hips. But every time it started to feel good, my eyelids began to shut, out of shyness or habit, and my father's face would appear. My father's face, close up, with its wrinkles and uneven landscape, the cracks, dilated pores, the rigid grey hairs. His face, or his voice. *Your head too heavy for you?* The kinds of phrases we recall, as though the past held only events of no importance.

But ordinary things can leave deeper, more painful impressions than dramatic events, even if it's just how you're supposed to cook an egg or how hot you like your coffee. I stayed at my father's for a few months before I left for Montreal, and my cat gave birth to a litter of kittens. I thought they would be good company, four cats running through the house, but he said he hated them and threatened to drown them in the toilet every time I went out, so I was relieved to quickly find homes for two of them. The day the kittens were adopted, my father wasn't himself. He kept picking them up to hold them and pet them, and I had to yank them out of his hands to give them to the two waiting couples. When I shut the door behind them, he started to cry. I wondered whether it was because of the cats or how abrupt I'd been. Maybe in my gesture he'd sensed the contempt I'd had for him for the past few years, my certainty that he was unable to take care of anyone. Later that evening, he asked me not to give away the other two kittens. He wanted to keep them. This story too is quite ordinary, but it cuts me to the quick. I see my hands moving in slow motion, grabbing the kittens from his arms to give to strangers, and my father's grey-blue eyes misting over. I can't undo the act or replace it. It's added to a list of what I remember of him. Not a list of acts of love or happy memories. Memory is thankless. A list of gestures, words and moments that should have gone differently.

/ 5

On the corner of my street, a small crowd has gathered around an old woman. I stop and pretend to look for my keys in my bag. I try to listen to see what's going on. I can't make out the conversations clearly, but a familiar smell hits me. Smells are not traces left behind; they conjure up the past exactly as it was, emotions and decor intact. As I'm thinking this, I realize the door to the old woman's apartment is open. I know exactly what I'd find if I stuck my head in: a home being emptied out. Open cardboard boxes strewn across the floor, garments—dress pants, shirts, ties, jackets—taken out from under their plastic and laid on the bed, big black garbage bags next to the clothes horse filled with everything too tattered or too personal to be given away or sold: broken objects, clothes and slips and socks stretched out or full of holes, shoes worn down at the heels. There would be a mattress leaning against the wall. There would be men taking the stove and the washer for scrap. There would be this smell, a sourness like sadness or sickness, and a bloodstained rag in a plastic bucket. Words would be floating around the rooms to give grief a consensual form. All this, I know. When my father died, the same smell seeped from his house as we emptied it out.

Sometimes, when I start thinking that Martin and I could stay together for a while longer, I imagine myself a widow. Martin's been gone a week, a month, three years, ten. The pain dulls with time; I make a new life—I like that expression, it makes life seem like a bed that can be freshened with new sheets whenever we choose. I'm almost fifty. Sometimes when I'm alone in the afternoons, I take out the album with photos of our life together, I sit on a wooden chair with a brown cushion and I turn the pages, wondering if I could have been happy all those years with only him. I stop at the photo I took of Martin in Paris when we first started dating; I place two fingers on his face as if they were a person's legs. My fingers trace his faint wrinkles and circle his eyes, following the length of his nose. If they slip, they'll fall right into his mouth, swallowed into the black hole between his teeth. But they don't. They pause on Martin's lips and I hear his voice murmur something about my eyes. I turn around and scan the room. But there's no one. I look at the photo of Martin again. "When you looked at me," he says without moving his lips, "your eyes never really saw who I was." And I answer, "Of course I saw you." He replies, "Your eyes looked at me as if searching for something that might have been there before." "Before what?" I ask. And we laugh, remembering that old argument, one we'd later talked about often, as we'd always been able to do with our arguments once they were over. Then Martin stops laughing. "Before me." When I play this scene over in my mind, I'm sitting in a kitchen with beige or brown walls and lace in the windows framed by orange curtains like in photos of the kitchens of my childhood. I look at Martin's picture and wonder if I loved him enough in the day-to-day, and I think I'd be right to imagine his ghost saying no.

"You don't realize it, but you never really gave us a chance to work things out."

I say no, I don't realize. And then he asks if it's because I was afraid of betraying my father that things between us reached a turning point. And I say, "What turning point?" and then, "No, no, that's not the reason."

Then I hear the front door, the kids coming back from school. They throw their bags to the floor and go thundering down the hall. Martin starts to leave. "Wait, Martin, don't go," I say. But his face has disappeared from the photo. In its place, a sentence: *How much do the dead really need the living?* I take the words as a reproach, from Martin to me, someone who has always put the dead first.

The kids come into the kitchen, toss me a hello and grab a chunk of cake from the still-warm piece on the table before I can tell them to wash their hands. I close the photo album and put it back between the cookbooks, dole out unwanted kisses. I drape the dish towel over the back of the chair and watch the second hand move across the face of the clock. It's not that Martin was my only love, but that the dead always win against the living.

/ 6

After my parents separated, my mother reorganized the photo albums. There are almost no photos left of my father now, just a silhouette in the background here and there, or his back. No one flipping through would be able to guess which of the men was the father of the little girls pictured. Once in a while, my mother says, "I wish I'd never met him," and it feels as though our existence becomes brittle, my sisters' and mine, and soon it could be us banished from the photos. But I'm being dramatic. My mother loves us too much to blot us from her life story.

Maybe one day I'll sort through my own photos and make an album that preserves the version of the past I want to keep. That's why it's important to take lots of pictures, and often. Not only to be able to remember. But for all the possible ways they can be arranged.

When I know enough about my future with Martin to create that definitive album, I'll sort through my photos. But for the moment, I can't part with any. Maybe I'm simply afraid of forgetting faces. Even the blurry shots help me with my prosopagnosia—such a pretty word for a neurological disorder that makes certain faces impossible to recognize. It was so bad with my ex that I made a point of arriving early to our dates so I wouldn't have to search for him in the crowd. Once, while I was waiting outside the metro, a man approached me smiling and I jumped into his arms, ready to kiss him, just as my boyfriend was walking toward me, clearly unimpressed.

But I always recognize Martin. I know his features as well as any landscape from my childhood. It sounds silly, but it's exactly that: his face is a familiar landscape, a lasting imprint. Sometimes I wonder if it's because there's something in his eyes so reminiscent of my father's passport photo. In it, my father is staring straight ahead with a mix of anger and sadness, as though he already knows he is getting his passport for a trip he will never take, and that it will be my fault. It's the last picture taken of him. A year before he died.

Martin never looks at me that way, as though his unhappiness is my fault. But in the Paris photo in the imaginary album I'll compile after his death, Martin almost has the look of someone readying himself for a great deal of suffering, even though he's too young to know it. You can see it most in the corners of his eyes and mouth. For now, it's a beautiful photograph of him. I'll discover plenty of narrative potential in the next twenty years, or maybe thirty or even forty, when our love will have taken its definitive form, and Martin will either be dead or bitter at having been loved so poorly for so long.

/ 7

Magritte has invaded the neighbourhood. Prints of his work are pasted on all the cement pillars outside the metro-station kiosk, low-quality black-and-white photocopies. I stop in front of a print of *The Red Model*, take a marker out of my bag and write, *This is not my father's head.* "That's pretty funny," says a voice next to me. I turn and it's a man around thirty, handsome face, brown hair, who looks like a musician or someone soliciting monthly donations for Greenpeace. He asks me if he can take the poster for his apartment. I pull it off the pillar, roll it up and hand it to him. He thanks me and we both walk toward the market without knowing who is following whom. I buy some meat for a roast, mushrooms, potatoes, eggs, bacon, basil, tomatoes, garlic, a wedge of sheep's milk cheese, milk, strawberries. The guy doesn't buy anything. The conversation flows easily, and we talk about existential things rarely discussed even between good friends. Or never at all, if you never meet the right people. When I finish my shopping, he walks with me toward my place as though we both know where we're headed.

I end up saying I'm home a few houses from mine. He hands me my bags, rips off the corner of a cigarette packet and scrawls his name on it. "Seriously though, call me," he says. I answer with a smile, the feeling that my stomach is full of warm water, a pleasant sensation, and turn around and take a few steps toward the house. Then I imagine him in the morning, feet slipping into his slippers stowed under the bed to go make the coffee—and then, emptiness again.

I arrive in front of my building, my arms full of grocery bags, which I switch to my left hand so I can check the mailbox with my right. Nothing. The door squeaks when I open it. Martin hasn't called all day. I leave the bags on the floor, walk down the dark hallway. I push open the door to my bedroom. Inside, it's quiet and still.

Marguerite Duras lived all alone in a big house in Neauphle-le-Château, not far from the village where my father grew up. She wrote, "Solitude is the thing without which one does nothing," and she listened to the floors creak in her two-storey house. I don't like the solitude of big houses because it's never a peaceful solitude. It's one inhabited by endless rooms you keep checking to be sure no one is hiding there. I don't even like the solitude of my two-room apartment. I turn the TV on in one room, the radio in the other, and I do the dishes, vacuum, water the plants, make a cake, make plans, schedule doctor's appointments, on a loop. And when that's not enough, I grab my coat and go out, in the hopes that a glance from a stranger will prove that all this—washing, dressing, eating, changing the sheets, living—isn't for nothing.

Sometimes I stop at a café to read. I sit at a small table, preferably facing away from the other customers, but close enough to catch bits of conversation. It feels like at any point I could turn around and give my thoughts on the baby's bedroom, Paule's friendship with this Marc guy, or maybe just to nod my head while blowing on my hot chocolate as I listen to the woman saying she sees right through so-and-so's game, and she isn't the kind to fall for it.

/ 8

In the living room, I put on the Italian Concerto in F Major, BWV 971. I had to turn up the bass. It's a bad recording; the piano scrapes the notes and violently hammers out the chords. Next, the Sonata No. 3 in C major, BMV 1005. I like to think Bach gave these works licence-plate numbers because he was fond of cars and uncomfortable with emotion. But that's exactly what I enjoy about Bach: the raw emotion. The higher I turn up the bass, the more I like Bach. I like Bach when he's crackly and saturated.

I've finally opened the box where I keep what I have left of my father's things. As I suspected, the pipe wasn't in it, but his pocket knife was there and a Ziploc bag with a passport inside and the Magritte postcard. I took the passport out of the bag and opened it to the photo page. I didn't look at the other pages, all the empty pages for all the trips my father never took, the trip to Canada he never took to see me. My sister Christelle had been helping him plan it. She'd called, and I was against the idea. Having him stay in my apartment, living with him, for two days or for a week, was unimaginable. But just one trip, Christelle had insisted. Looking back, I don't know how I could have refused him that.

In his passport photo, my father is forty-six years old, but no one would ever believe it. They would say he looked twenty years older. But they'd also say he looked kind. His friend Philippe told me he had a heart as big as a camper van. Philippe never saw the photo. Or the blank passport. The pain in those eyes. The photo conveys all the suffering my father accumulated throughout his life, especially in those last years. It's a photo where he asks anyone whose eyes meet his—and often that's me—why he was so alone, the kind of image you'd rather forget, but you can't, because it's the only one you have. If I'd had a smart phone when he died, I'd have taken a photo of him at the morgue. It would have been more bearable to look at.

I put the passport aside and looked at Martin's minuscule eyes in the photo-booth pictures on my desk, the four black-and-white versions of our love. In the first two, he's in profile, looking at me while I look away. In the third, he's kissing me. In the fourth, Martin is staring straight ahead. It was startling to see his expression, in the same format as my father's passport picture—the same composition, same pose, same beard, but such different eyes. My father's eyes are hollowed out by sadness and anger, drained, while Martin's are full, full of things he wants to communicate, sadness included, but other things too. It's as though Martin's eyes hadn't yet been spun dry, something I hadn't dared notice.

It gave me an idea. I went to my bedroom to get my markers. I took out a black one, and red, blue, yellow, brown. I drew handlebar moustaches on my father's photo, a top hat and a jacket collar. I coloured over his mouth with a big smile, added black spots to his nose, blue on his eyelids. I couldn't stop. I drew makeup on Martin too. I was on a roll, so I took the Magritte postcard from the plastic bag, opened it up and read each sentence one by one, as though they'd been written by someone other than me and it wasn't my father who had read them. Some of the lines I read aloud: they were pretty and I let myself believe the person they were intended for had cried with joy on reading them. Then I placed the thick black marker at the end of the first line, on the P in Papa, and slid it across the letters one by one until I arrived at the end of the word. It gave me chills. I wondered whether things can exist after there's nothing left, not a trace.

I got to the next line, rested my marker on the start of it, on the I. *I'm sending you this Magritte painting. It's an excuse to write to you, because I've been wanting to for such a long time…* I slid the marker over one letter after the other. I wondered if my father would continue to exist after this, when there wasn't anything left of him, and how I'd continue to exist when I could no longer place myself at the end of his story, since it would be completely erased. Will I have to reinvent my lineage?

My hand hovered over the next line, ready to cross it out, and the line after that, and the next, until the left side was covered in black lines, and I did the same with the right, until the card was no longer really a card a girl had sent her father before he died. And then I put on a Fever Ray CD, because a storm was brewing outside.

/ 9

The phone keeps ringing, but I don't answer. I think about my father. I think about how we can get up every morning, work, eat, talk, smile, but still be dead. The phone rings. I tell myself that's what killed him: the days dwindling, his eyes searching through the window, the hours bleaching away, and before long we're talking without really listening, about your day and mine, about our schedules, starting sentences with the time of day and a list of activities, or maybe that's not it at all.

The phone rings. I remember a gesture my father would make, around other people. He'd go over to my mother and ask for a kiss, or touch one of her breasts. Unsubtle and unromantic. She'd have to wriggle free, "Stop, Mario," under her breath but without conviction, and she'd laugh, as if humour were the only defence mechanism she had to keep him at bay.

The phone rings. I don't want to die like he did. After being too afraid, after giving up too much. I don't want silence to set in once the words we've used to fill our conversations have been emptied of all substance. I don't want to die with regrets as heavy as a shovelful of wet snow. I don't want to give in to that life just because it's easier, a safer bet. I sit with my back against the door and talk to Martin's photo. I tell him how I have eyes everywhere, at the tip of my fingers, on my stomach, my breasts, the soles of my feet. It will take so many landscapes to satisfy all those eyes, I tell him.

Someone knocks at the door and I don't answer. I remember something my dad said a few weeks after my mom left: "I'm going to ask her to come back." I was about to say something about roses, restaurants, dances, the movies, but then he said he couldn't manage without her, the dirty laundry was piling up, the house was filthy, and I thought at that moment how I never wanted to be loved like that, out of need. But isn't it always a bit like that? Do we ever really know, when we love, if it's for the right reasons, and in the right way?

There's a knock at the door.

"Open up, Céline."

The key turns in the lock. The door opens a crack, my slumped body blocking it. Martin tries to pop his head through the gap, looking to see what's in the way. It's me, sitting on the floor.

"I don't want you to end up like my dad, Martin."

"Don't be ridiculous," he says. "Come on, move out of the way."

He steps over me and through my father's ghost, which had settled in the hallway to keep me company. I don't say anything to Martin. He goes to the kitchen, opens the window and the balcony door, sets a paper bag on the table, runs some water, moves the dishes aside, then comes back, bends down, puts his hands on my shoulders, then around my back, pulls me toward him and holds me. I hear the coffee whistling on the stove, and Martin asks if I want to move in with him. It's hard to believe but I'm happy. That's what I tell him between sobs. And I say yes. And then I tell him I love him. But just so you know, I'm saying *I love you* for this exact second, not the next.

CHANGEMENTS DE DOMICILE

Le changement de domicile dont la déclaration n'est en aucun cas obligatoire, est mentionné sur demande faite au Commissaire de police ou, à défaut, au Maire du nouveau domicile.

Nouveau domicile

Le   Le Commissaire de police
                                                    Le Maire

Nouveau domicile

Le   Le Commissaire de police
                                                    Le Maire

RÉPUBLIQUE FRANÇAISE

SOUS-PRÉFECTURE
DE RAMBOUILLET

CARTE NATIONALE
D'IDENTITÉ

Valable dix années à partir
de la date d'émission

N° 334461

TIMBRE FISCAL
P 15,00

XV65661

Né le   1ER JANVIER 1957
à   THIVERVAL GRIGNON
                    -78-

NATIONALITÉ FRANÇAISE

Taille   1M76   Signature du titulaire
Signes   /
particuliers
Domicile   8 Rue de la Fontaine
                    Quenette
                    78 GARANCIERES

Fait le   9 JUIN 1987
par

LE SOUS-PRÉFET
Pour le Sous-Préfet
Le Secrétaire Général

HANDWRITING ANALYSIS

Sylvie Chermet-Carroy
Graphologist

Paris, June 19, 2014

The first thing apparent in the signature you submitted for analysis was that it is relatively large despite the fact it is on an identity card; generally in this context a signature is scaled down to fit the limited space. Here we have an individual who has used all the space provided, or more than provided, in fact. That tells us this is someone who wants to take all the space offered to them in their life as well. We know that for starters.

The pressure is also revealing. It translates how we live and how our energy manifests itself. Here, there's a good amount of pressure; the person is energetic. But on closer examination, the pressure is also irregular. For some loops, the downstroke is much lighter. It is almost as though there were a contrast between an immense sense of moral conviction and a touch of vulnerability or doubt, moments when the individual ultimately hesitates in asserting themselves. At least, the way this person engages and asserts themselves is inconstant, even if it is not evident from the outside. It's something happening internally.

The signature as a whole is ascending: the letters are horizontal and ascending, which signifies energy and enthusiasm. And there is something very interesting here—the signature has completely gone outside the border of the card, as though the signature line finishes on the table, a rare example, especially on an ID card, where people tend to remain inside the space provided. We can see the signature was well positioned to start, then the person gave up and figured they would do as they liked. This is an individual who knows how to set boundaries, and how to respect societal expectations, but doesn't see it through. At their core, they are in revolt against anything constraining, any framework or imposed limits. Anything that labels or hinders. On the surface, there is an acceptance of the need to play a part, not cause problems, but deep down they despise it. The person is a rebel. That much is extremely clear.

The stroke continues to the right, indefinitely. In my work with children's drawings, lines that extend beyond page boundaries are significant. Here, it is rightward. The right represents what's to come, the direction we are moving in: progress, the future, and also the unknown. And what is particularly interesting in this person's signature is that there is exuberance, but at the same time a certain level of reserve, because it seems care has been taken with the first letters, the movement is controlled.

It could even be said there is a wariness in the restrained movement in the first two letters. They can almost be considered a logo separate from the signature. A small blank space separates them from the rest, followed by tremendous movement toward the future. This is someone who wants to be cautious, but whose only aspiration deep down is to charge ahead.

The desire to charge ahead doesn't necessarily show optimism. Some shapes are nearly black even though the ink is blue. We can make out a *j* and a *b*. It is common for letters to appear in signatures that do not exist in the name itself; it is curious why the unconscious has caused a certain form to emerge, such as a letter, out of a spontaneous motion. In the signature provided, the person has written a *b* instead of the *h* in their name, created from the downstroke and a small black blot in the loop, which evokes self-contemplation, concerns, a person who dwells on problems, a little anxiety—restrained anxiety, since the stroke turns inward on itself. Instead of charging ahead, the person calculates, to ensure they have done things right.

The *h* is related to sociability, among other things. It is how we commune with the universe and with the world. The letter *h* tells us how we relate to others, and also about our relationship to ourselves. Being part of a group requires a minimum of self-esteem. As for the *b*, it is a meditation and reflection, a ripening of ideas. The person is not spontaneously outgoing; their sociability is studied, deliberate. This is not to say it is artificial or contrived, as the overall movement of the signature is quite sincere. But maybe the person is not very sociable. Deep down, they know effort is needed to create social connections. What is apparent is that sociability is something on this individual's mind or in their considerations.

Other letters are missing. This is something we see frequently with signatures. Since signatures are meant to be written quickly, the more often they are reproduced, the more likely they are to distort. Certain forms will combine with others and the result can be a drawing, a sculpture, abstract art. But every letter represented in the signature but not present in the name provides us with information.

For example, in this signature we find a large *j*. The *j* relates to action, and to sexuality, in the broad sense of the term. It's also an assertion of the way we think, of what we attribute meaning to in our lives. It is an expression of dedication and assertiveness. The person is affirming their potential, their complexity, their identity. We tend to see the *j* in more authoritative individuals. But here it is gentler: a strong *j* but with fluid forms. There is a noted balance here between the feminine and the masculine. Perhaps it is slightly more masculine, given the energy in the descender (the portion of a letter that drops below the line, as with a *j*), and then there is a strong movement toward

the right. But there is also something that can be described as feminine, full of sensitivity and emotion, revealed mainly in the instability
of the stroke; it shows more internal nuance. Perhaps this sensitivity
has not entirely been explored. Artistic inclination, for instance. I
think this individual must be sensitive to art, given their sensuality,
but without a concrete outlet. Perhaps they enjoy crafting beautiful
objects out of wood, or perhaps they like improving the aesthetics of
certain objects, because they like handling these objects. The writing
stroke is also quite sensual: thick and wide. The individual is someone
who wants to enjoy what life has on offer, who knows how to savour
life's sweet moments. The medial portion of the writing is gentle and
completely round.

There's a gentleness, but also some anger visible in the highly
impulsive movement driving to the right. Something about the person is difficult to pinpoint. This person keeps a lot inside, they have
a lot of reserve, they are self-contained, but all of that ends up being
expressed as anger. We can see this in the pressure of the stroke moving
upward, very fast and with heavy pressure, and in how it diverges in
an unexpected direction, unexpected even for this individual. Like
anger. An accumulation of anger. But there is no ill will; we see this in
how there are no dots in the writing. There is only roundness, other
than the mysterious stroke that pushes outward and a small dot above
what I'm calling the *j*, but the dot is toward the sky, toward the mind,
like an ideal.

There is, however, a certain hesitancy between what I view as a *b*
and the *e:* there is a small blot where the individual pressed into the
paper. When you sign in a fluid motion, it gives a clean stroke. This
person is attentive to their behaviour. The gesture of hesitation shows
a lack of confidence, or a hesitation as to what the person really wants
to do, especially given the lovely propulsive energy pushing them forward, perhaps even too far, which can lead to a questioning of whether
to act or hold back. We can suppose that they fear not being able to
stop once they have started something, whether that is a decision, a

project, romantic love or a creation. Once it has begun, they don't know where it will lead, like their anger.

The person's origins are hard to discern. It seems they want to be straightforward—someone who wants a simple life and who does not suffer pretense. There is a certain simplicity in their way of being, their life choices, because that is what suits them, deeply, rather than by design. But I cannot tell you much more than that.

Characters

THE MOTHER, *Christelle, Céline and Élodie's mother*
CHRISTELLE, *the eldest*
CÉLINE, *the middle child*
ÉLODIE, *the youngest*
PHILIPPE, *a childhood friend and Mario's ex-brother-in-law*
MARC, *the mother's brother*
ANNETTE, *the mother's sister, Philippe's ex-wife*
JEANNE, *Mario's sister*
FRANÇOIS, *Jeanne's husband*
YANN, *the mother's partner*
A FRIEND OF CÉLINE'S
A NEIGHBOUR
ANOTHER NEIGHBOUR

Families are governed by codes of conduct, a language, what we can say and what's forbidden. We learn compliance through mimicry. There are certain questions we don't dare ask, since no one asked them before us. We each end up believing in some deep secret that, if it were revealed, would tear the family apart. But that's not it. It's not the secret that's the threat, it's the question we never ask. If we did, none of the answers would reveal anything new, but we would no longer be able to cling to our own little narratives.

I had written out a fairly long list of people I wanted to speak with while I was in France, and my notebook was filled with phone numbers and addresses. I was afraid, and I kept putting off the calls.

The first interviews were especially hard. I had this naive idea that I would be leading my family to a point of no return. But I wasn't brave enough to break the silence. I didn't even manage to make us relive the events; we barely pieced them back together. So I returned three years later for a second series of interviews. I wanted to talk to the same people, ask them the same questions. They would be free to correct the text as they read it, on camera.

Few were willing. Some had died; others refused. Among those who agreed, memories had softened, the bitterness swept under happy anecdotes. I took the dead, the refusals and the pleasant sentiments. I did what I could with them.

Everything starts there. The interviews are not evidence. They don't reveal the truth of an event, only the speaker's relationship to it.

Scene 1

PHILIPPE, CÉLINE

They planned to meet in the parking lot of a supermarket near her mother's apartment. He spots Céline first and motions to her as he steps out of the car.

PHILIPPE: *(From afar)* Do you ever look like your little sister! I thought you were her.

He calls her sister "la petite." And the term of endearment amplifies the distance between Céline and the rest of her family. Time, exile have rendered her "the one who looks like la petite."

CÉLINE: I guess I do, don't I?

She asks if it's okay to call him by his first name.

PHILIPPE: Course. You're like a daughter to me. I was there when you were born, just about.

He enfolds her in arms tattooed with anchors and faded blue names. She smiles. Hidden under her smile and good manners are all the ways in which she resembles this man.

PHILIPPE: My daughter lives right there, in one of those beehive apartments. But I'm rarely here. I live in Pontchartrain now. Between there and the South.

CÉLINE: Do you like it better in Pontchartrain?

45

PHILIPPE: Nah…that's not it.

CÉLINE: Bad memories?

PHILIPPE: Yeah. It's too much now.

CÉLINE: What's too much?

PHILIPPE: No one calls anymore. My boys don't call me.

The week before, Céline had visited Annette, Greg and Alex. The two boys, her cousins, told her they were done seeing their father, he had caused them too much pain: "He only shows up when he needs something from us."

PHILIPPE: When he turned eighteen, Greg didn't want to see me anymore. I figured he's at that age, he has a girlfriend, other things to do. Then Alex decided to stop coming too when he turned eighteen. I went over to Annette's once to talk to them. They weren't home, she said, but I could hear their footsteps upstairs. "Tell them if they don't give a shit about me, I don't give a shit about them either." That's what I said to her.

CÉLINE: But it wasn't true.

PHILIPPE: No. *(He flicks his cigarette on the ground.)* I don't know why they don't want to see me anymore.

They also said, "There was already a lot of other stuff. But when your dad died, that was the last straw. He didn't come to the funeral. And we haven't forgiven him for that." Céline searches for the words to let Philippe know what she knows without betraying her cousins' trust.

CÉLINE: Maybe you did something they felt hurt by? Maybe you weren't really there for them at some point?

PHILIPPE: No. No, it happened all at once. When they turned eighteen. Before then, they used to visit.

He lights another cigarette. He says, "I smoke, but I don't drink. That stuff killed your dad." He's starting with the ending.

PHILIPPE: He told me he wanted to see my brother. I called, I said, "Dominique, you need to come right away." I couldn't say why, because I was with your dad, but I told him it was important. He came. When he was leaving, my brother said to me, "Did you see all that blood on the floor?" "I didn't notice." "He must've wiped it up, but you can still see it." I called your sisters. I told them they had to bring your dad to the hospital. That it was an emergency. That's the last time I saw him.

CÉLINE: You didn't get the chance to see him again?

PHILIPPE: My stepmom died, and I had to go to the South. I didn't really know what to do. Your dad had surgery. I was worried. "It's just some tests," my girlfriend reassured me. "They'll find out what's wrong and he'll be okay." That's not what happened. I would've liked to visit him in the hospital. They told me it was family only. "But I'm pretty much family..." "We'll see what we can do." And then they told me he was dead. I didn't see him again. *(He is crying.)* I couldn't go to the funeral.

CÉLINE: Because you were in the South?

PHILIPPE: Because it was too much. I couldn't come back for two and a half months. I stayed down there. I couldn't do it. He was my best friend. *(He wipes his tears with the back of his hand.)* I'm sick, you know. My head's a mess. I'm diabetic. And there's something wrong with one of my arteries.

CÉLINE: You should see a doctor.

PHILIPPE: I don't have the guts for that. And…I don't want to know. All my buddies are dead. Internal bleeding, cancer. I've had it. Your dad was my best friend. We sure had some wild times.

CÉLINE: What's hardest for you? That you're lonely?

PHILIPPE: It's not that. He's right here. *(He taps his chest.)* He's always here with me. Even if he didn't believe in God, it's still God who called him back. No, I'm not lonely. He's still here with me. He's always with you too.

Scene 2

CÉLINE, CHRISTELLE

Christelle is at the head of the bed, her back resting against the bedroom wall. Her smooth blond hair is loose and falls over her shoulders. She's beautiful and smiling, a slightly anxious look on her face. The sheets of paper are spread out in front of her. She hasn't read them. She's listening to Céline explain how the second interview will go. "So I had to cut a few things, because we talked for over three hours. If it's okay with you, I'll ask you the questions and you answer as if you were doing a casting call. You don't have to follow the script exactly. If you want to change something, because you don't remember saying it, you can. Or if there's anything you forgot to say the first time." She adds that there are a few trick questions: ones she hasn't asked before. Christelle can answer them however she likes.

"I'll put the camera here." Céline sets up the camera on a tripod a metre away from her sister. It's a classic shot, medium close-up, at a slight angle. From time to time, Christelle leans out of the frame to grab a cup of tea resting on the floor; she reappears, brings the cup to her lips, then bends over again to rest it on the carpet next to the bed. She tells her sister that memory is deceptive, that by correcting herself after the fact like this, she might well be erasing the truth. On camera, we don't see Céline's face as she answers, "Exactly."

CÉLINE: Last time we started talking right away, and I forgot to ask you to introduce yourself, so I'll do that now. Can you introduce yourself?

CHRISTELLE: My name is Christelle Huyghebaert.

CÉLINE: And what's your connection to Papa?

CHRISTELLE: He's... He was my dad.

CÉLINE: And I'm adding a question I asked Élodie the first time around, but not you. How do you see my project?

CHRISTELLE: *(Laughing)* How do I see it? I see it as an art project. And I think it's also work you need so you can grieve, and reclaim someone who, in the end, had gotten away from you or who you'd distanced yourself from.

CÉLINE: Do you feel like you're done grieving?

CHRISTELLE: *(Hesitating for a moment)* I guess I don't fully know what that means...

CÉLINE: That it doesn't feel painful anymore?

CHRISTELLE: If that's what it means...then yes, I'm done grieving. I didn't deal with my grief until the year after Papa died, but it happened eventually. Before that I was in denial. *(Short pause)* In the end, it's really whatever your survival mechanisms are. Mine are to set things aside for a while.

CÉLINE: For the funeral?

CHRISTELLE: Funerals are a ritual. It's not one that feels right to me, but it's a social thing. You have to be there. If you're not at your father's funeral, people are going to judge you.

CÉLINE: I don't remember who told me about going to a wake. The body was in a room for a whole week. *(She grimaces.)* The immediate family stayed with the body. And the extended family dealt with the paperwork, organized the funeral, and even the grocery shopping, cooking and cleaning. Over those few days, being with the body in that room, the family got used to the death and could let the person go more easily.

CHRISTELLE: I don't think that would feel right to me at all.

CÉLINE: No?

CHRISTELLE: I need to…escape a little.

CÉLINE: How so?

CHRISTELLE: I need to forget, and shift my focus to something else.

CÉLINE: Shift it back to a routine?

CHRISTELLE: Yes. For instance, after Papa died, I went out a lot, saw lots of friends. I didn't feel like grieving then.

CÉLINE: But it caught up to you?

CHRISTELLE: Yes, but I think it's less intense when it catches up to me later. *(She rests the papers on her knees and looks at her sister.)* At the same time, I'm on the verge of tears right now, so I'm not sure if I'm completely done. But I guess I live with the weight and the pain that's still there. I don't know that you ever really get over it completely.

At the end of the interview, a few seconds before Céline stops the camera, Christelle says, off-script, "I don't know whether Mom is really ready to redo her interview. I'm not really sure you should force her." She phrases this gently but her expression is resolute, so much so that Céline feels the guilt between her ribs, just under her breastbone—a feeling that's becoming harder and harder to shut off. "I know," is all she answers.

Scene 3

CÉLINE, THE MOTHER

Céline goes to join her mother in the kitchen. She's asked her to read two or three pages of the interview before deciding. The mother makes coffee in abrupt, concentrated movements. She avoids looking at Céline, who is trying to make conversation to put her at ease.

CÉLINE: Remember that morning we did the interview? You told me you'd had a nightmare.

THE MOTHER: I was looking after three kids in a room with all the doors blocked. The place was a mess: the cupboard doors were wide open, packets of cake ripped apart, crumbs scattered across the counters. And I was trapped there.

CÉLINE: Did you make a connection at the time between the dream and the questions I wanted to ask you about Papa?

THE MOTHER: Yes, because the past is always within us. We might think it's far away, but it's always here. We live with it.

CÉLINE: And then later, when I asked what time was good for us to do the interview, you said—

Her mother is leaning over the papers on the table and, without sitting down, she starts reading.

THE MOTHER: Listen, I've thought about it, and I don't want to.

CÉLINE: This project is really important to me, Mom; I need to know my father.

THE MOTHER: You did know him.

CÉLINE: Not as a person, not as a man. I only knew him as a father.

THE MOTHER: Children don't need to know their parents that way.

CÉLINE: I do though. I was living in Montreal when he died. There's a lot I wasn't around for.

THE MOTHER: Then talk to your sisters.

CÉLINE: They didn't know him like you did.

Her mother straightens up again. The coffee's ready. She pours it into two cups, her hands a little unsteady, and brings them into the living room. Céline follows, holding the papers and an audio recorder.

CÉLINE: You said, "I can't do this," and started crying. I grabbed my phone and left the house, slammed the door on my way out. I went for a walk to try to calm down, but it didn't work. I suddenly couldn't see anymore why I'd gotten it into my head to do this in the first place, to come here for these interviews, and I wanted to call it all off, get back on the plane to Montreal and forget the whole thing. I called Martin. I told him the interviews weren't going the way I'd hoped. He said I could stop any time I wanted. I stopped crying. I knew he was wrong, I couldn't stop now. And then we talked about what we always do when one of us is away: we compared the weather, I asked about his cat, I admitted that bringing my big red coat had been a bad idea because it was too warm and not dressy enough for Paris. When I hung up, I kept walking until my anger wore down, and also my fear of bothering you all and taking up too much space. And I went back. When I got here, we hugged. You told me you'd gotten scared we'd never talk again, and I told you that was silly. We stayed in the entryway, a few feet from the front door, while I told you about the project. I explained that I didn't remember what Papa had told us about his childhood. "I can do that," you said, "I just can't talk to you about us as a couple." You started crying again. "I'm sure there were lots of happy moments too, but all that's been erased. It's too much," you told me.

"I understand," I said. "You can say no to any of the questions you aren't comfortable with. You decide. I just want to know who he was."

"Okay, that I can do. You know, maybe, little by little, I'll open up. If it hadn't been for your grandpa—he's the one who ruined everything for us."

We came to sit down here, you on the sofa and me facing you in the chair. It was awkward with the red light glowing on the audio recorder. We spoke in voices we were trying to pass off as our own.

Céline edits her transcript: "as our real voices." She sips her coffee. It's boiling hot, just the way she likes it.

CÉLINE: Do you feel as nervous today as you did the first time?

THE MOTHER: No, no. But I don't want to do the interview again. *(Pause)* I did it the last time, but it's too much.

Long silence.

THE MOTHER: I know you're annoyed with me, but…

CÉLINE: No, Mom, of course not. I understand…

THE MOTHER: If you really need me to, then I'll do it.

CÉLINE: We won't do it. I know I've already asked a lot of you.
Her mother doesn't let her finish, just puts her arms around her. With a shaky voice, she thanks her. Céline's body remains still. She wishes she had the decency to stop now. The guilt she's dragged around with her since the start of the project is a small, prickly green ball striking her skin in short, repeated movements, always the same spots, until the slightest contact becomes unbearable.

CÉLINE: There are a few things I forgot to ask you last time, and I wish I hadn't. Would you be willing to answer them in writing?

THE MOTHER: *(Tired)* Yes, of course. Not now. But later I can.

Céline takes the pages from the table and pulls out the ones with the new questions. She still hopes to uncover events that will make the story less banal. She's thinking of a passage in Suite for Barbara Loden *where Nathalie Léger tries to explain to her mother why she's having so much trouble writing Loden's biography. Her mother is surprised: "How difficult can it be to tell a story simply?" And Nathalie Léger answers with a question: "What does it mean, 'to tell a story simply'?" And the mother confidently "mentions* Anna Karenina, Lost Illusions *and* Madame Bovary; *she says it means a beginning, a middle and an end, especially an end."*

Scene 4

ÉLODIE, CÉLINE, CHRISTELLE

Since the project began, the most significant things have happened off-camera. With Élodie, it's a story about a fight between Aunt Jeanne and the mother that starts before Céline has time to set up the camera on the tripod; the story just keeps going and going, like a bike with brakes that have given out.

ÉLODIE: Mom and I went to Jeanne's. Mom wanted to tell her about the divorce and that we were moving. Papa was going to keep the house until he could find an apartment.

Jeanne didn't react the way the mother had hoped. She lost her temper, warned them she wouldn't be there to pick up the pieces this time. She'd taken her own father into her home until his death. She certainly wouldn't be doing the same for her brother. Maybe she hadn't been that explicit. But these are the words etched into Céline's memory when she thinks of this scene, which she didn't witness herself.

CÉLINE: Did you have time to read the interview this week?

ÉLODIE: I did. I went over it again carefully when I had some time alone.

Élodie holds the pages. She has crossed out certain passages and inserted others. The camera, placed randomly on the table, films her hands.

CÉLINE: You found mistakes?

ÉLODIE: No, it's just that I... Some of the things I said...

CÉLINE: You don't remember saying?

ÉLODIE: At all.

CÉLINE: You know you can take out anything you don't want published.

ÉLODIE: There are definitely certain sentences I really don't remember saying.

Élodie talks about the things she said three years before. Things she doesn't want anyone to remember, not even herself. Céline is seized with a coughing fit; each time she tries to answer her sister, a dry cough claws at the words in her throat and stifles them. She thinks about the sound quality of the recording—it's shot. What can you do... She leaves the dining room to get a glass of water and tries again to utter something intelligible, but it comes out as a wheeze. She finally manages to say something. The whole time, Élodie has been talking. She's speaking about a Michel Huyghebäert, who she met by coincidence when she was hospitalized.

ÉLODIE: From the little bit of research I've done, I know he was born in the same city as Grandpa, and they had the same mother. That's what I wrote in my letter to Jeanne. I remember writing that letter and going to leave it on her doorstep. I buzzed, then went down to the bottom of the stairs because I didn't want her to... I'd signed the letter, but... Anyway, no one ever brought it up with me.

Céline is having trouble following. Her sister is speaking too quickly.

CÉLINE: And this Michel, did you see him again?

ÉLODIE: Yeah, we met when I was at the cardiac rehabilitation centre. They mixed up our files and gave him my treatment by accident. That's when they told me there was someone with the same name on my floor, a Mr. Huyghebäert. When I saw him, I couldn't believe it: he was the spitting image of Grandpa, just younger. It was Grandpa, minus the drinking and sadness.

CÉLINE: What did he say?

ÉLODIE: "Incredible! You look just like my mother!" *(Laughs)* He's not in France very often, because his wife is Bosnian. He has two kids who really want to meet me. His daughter lives just outside Paris and the other one lives near Grenoble.

CÉLINE: So that would be Grandpa's brother?

ÉLODIE: Or his half-brother. It's unclear.

CÉLINE: He doesn't know his family either?

ÉLODIE: He knows who his mother is. He was the only child she'd acknowledged as her own when he reached legal age. She tried to reconnect with him. Apparently he was the youngest. She had a lot of regrets. He has photos of her, and he's met her a few times. But he didn't keep seeing her. It was too complicated, emotionally.

CÉLINE: And what about Grandpa, did you talk about him?

ÉLODIE: Michel doesn't know how many children she had. He

doesn't know his siblings. She gave them all up. But they have her last name. Michel's the only who kept the accent on the *a*. The others used the French spelling, without an accent, because she never acknowledged them.

Céline's ready to start. She has set up the shot: Élodie sitting on a wooden chair, wearing a pink cotton scarf.

CÉLINE: Right, I'll stop you there, because we need to get started or we'll be here all night. All set? You can add any corrections to the pages as we read through. *(Élodie nods, and Céline starts reading.)* Can you introduce yourself?

ÉLODIE: My name is Élodie Huyghebaert. I'm almost thirty-two.

CÉLINE: What's your connection to Papa?

ÉLODIE: He's my dad.

CÉLINE: You're saying that in present tense?

ÉLODIE: Yes, he's my Papa.

She says it in a little girl's voice, rounding out the a *sounds.*

CÉLINE: How do you see my project?

ÉLODIE: It's sort of a way for you to grieve, of talking about Papa and seeing the positive. It's not always easy to remember the good things, but you have to if you want to be able to live with the past.

Céline chokes on another cough. We hear footsteps moving away, then coming back, a series of swallows. Céline doesn't believe in it, the idea of looking back and trying to see the positive. She doesn't want to live everything over again.

CHRISTELLE (*Later, in a different conversation*): There are a lot of things that are still too much for me. The guilt. (*Silence*) I felt so guilty. (*Pause*) I think in any grieving process, you always feel guilty about something.

/

He's seventeen. He doesn't yet know that one day I'll be so much like him that he'll have to despise me just a little.

I asked people who didn't know my father to fill out a questionnaire about him, and left a quote to guide them:

It would help if you answered all items as best you can even if you are not absolutely certain or the item seems daft.

—Sophie Calle, "Psychological Assessment,"
based on an idea by Damien Hirst

1 of 9

/ PSYCHOLOGICAL PROFILE

Can you tell me in a few words who my father was?
A taciturn but loving man.

What did you like about him? What were his qualities?
His sense of curiosity and his ability to listen, from what I've heard.

And his faults?
Faults? I'd call them idiosyncrasies.

An anecdote?
I was struck by the fact he supposedly always had a copy of Thomas Bernhard's *Woodcutters* on him.

/ FAMILY HISTORY

Tell me about a few pivotal moments in his life, between his birth and death.

When he was little, he fell off his bicycle and broke his right arm.

As a teen, he thought about running away. As a young man, he read William Faulkner and Thomas Bernhard. As an adult, he didn't know who he was anymore, and he started drinking.

How did he meet my mother?
Walking along a canal.

How did he propose?
It was sudden. He had thought about it for a little while but blurted out the question in the heat of the moment.

What happened after?
The usual: a move to a new house, kids, work, boredom.

/ HISTORY OF HIS DEATH

Do you remember what he died of?
I'm not sure what he died of.

Did he know he was going to die?
Yes, he knew, and maybe he even wanted to.

Is there something that could have saved him?
The desire to live, quite simply.

Did he have a happy life?
In spite of everything, yes!

/ INTERVIEWEE'S PERSONAL HISTORY

Who are you?
I'm a reader, passionate about writing and the possible emergence of thought.

What is your connection to my father?
I can't really say there's a connection. More a curiosity.

Have you lost a parent? How do you live with that loss?
Not yet, but it won't be long, and knowing that isn't easy. It's something I think about all the time.

Do you have any comments?
What is it that makes you want to write a book about your father?

2 of 9

/ PSYCHOLOGICAL PROFILE

Can you tell me, in a few words, who my father was?
A sailor. Someone who was often away for work. He was a father who always hoped to spend more time with his wife and family, but whose work obligations kept him far away.

What did you like about him? What were his qualities?
I like the same thing about him that I liked about my own father: he didn't speak poorly of others. If he didn't like someone, he kept it to himself.

And his faults?
He spent too much time staring into the distance, imagining that tomorrow would be better. He wasn't present when he should have been.

An anecdote?
He had a really nice smile. He loved telling stories and making people laugh.

/ FAMILY HISTORY

Tell me about a few pivotal moments in his life, between his birth and death.
He considered the pivotal moments in his life to be the day he met your mother and when his kids were born, and that's what he'd always tell his friends. But what he really liked most was being out at sea with the crew, far from everything.

How did he meet my mother?
I think they met at a dance. It was kind of love at first sight. They both really loved dancing.

How did he propose?
They didn't know each other well. Your dad was already a sailor, and he asked your mother to marry him before he set off on a long voyage.

What happened after?
You came along not long after they were married. Maybe seven months later. He wasn't there to meet you.

/ HISTORY OF HIS DEATH

Do you remember what he died of?
He died of cancer. He was only fifty. At first, he didn't want you to know. He hid it from everyone, including himself. He died in just a few months.

Did he know he was going to die?
I think the part of him that didn't want to believe he was going to die was stronger than the part of him that knew he would.

Is there something that could have saved him?
I think if he'd accepted he was sick and gotten treatment earlier, he'd have had a better chance of getting better, or, at least, maybe he wouldn't have died so soon.

Did he have a happy life?
He had happy days. I no longer believe that life should be happy.

/ INTERVIEWEE'S PERSONAL HISTORY

Who are you?
I'm a visual artist. I live in Montreal.

What is your connection to my father?
My connection with your father is a fictional one. I remember that he died of cancer too young, like my father.

Have you lost a parent? How do you live with that loss?
My mother died very young, at twenty-six, when I was only six years old. My father died at fifty-eight. I was twenty-three. Death is very present in my life. The death of my mother permanently altered me; it shaped who I am. My father died just as we were starting to have an adult relationship and real conversations.

Do you have any comments?
Understanding that we'll die one day too is almost impossible for our brains to process—the idea that we'll no longer be here.

3 of 9

/ PSYCHOLOGICAL PROFILE

Can you tell me, in a few words, who my father was?
He was an incredibly sensitive man who you, your sisters and your
mom all loved very much. He had trouble saying how he felt, because
he was awkward with other people. And he was funny, half because he
liked to joke around and half in spite of himself, when he'd grumble
about everything and anything.

What did you like about him? What were his qualities?
I enjoyed his muttering, his old-fashioned views and his grumbling.
Thinking about him, I feel like he would have made me laugh, because
I'd probably have found him rough around the edges but endearing.
And I'm sure he was a smart man, and I admire intelligence in others.
I would have liked to learn from him—about his love of the land, how
to use my hands. If I'd spent time with him, I would have become
slightly more of a man.

And his faults?
I've partially listed them above. I think that if he had gone too far, his
prejudices and complaining would have gotten on my nerves, because
it would have reminded me how domineering parents can be.

An anecdote?
A saying: for every action, a disaster.

/ FAMILY HISTORY

Tell me about a few pivotal moments in his life, between his birth and death.

He was proud of himself when:

He gutted a pig for the first time. It was in front of his father. He wasn't afraid.

He made a friend jealous, at the age of twelve, by winning over the girl the friend liked. When, in fact, your dad could have cared less about the girl.

He got his first job shining shoes at the age of fourteen.

He knocked up your mother three times, even though the second time was an accident.

He bought a farm.

His three daughters were born.

He showed his daughters how to skin and gut a rabbit.

How did he meet my mother?

—

How did he propose?

He was a man of tradition. One sunny Sunday afternoon, he got down on one knee, offered her a modest ring and asked for her hand. She said yes. The two of them burst into tears. He felt manly for having proposed; she felt fulfilled since she'd always dreamed of being proposed to. They'd idealized a moment for reasons that had nothing to do with the other person's experience.

What happened after?

He saw a toad in the grass and grabbed it, and, as a joke, he tossed it at your mother. She got mad, they fought a bit, then went home again. Then he drank a beer and she did some knitting.

/ HISTORY OF HIS DEATH

Do you remember what he died of?
He died of cirrhosis-related complications caused by nosocomial bacteria.

Did he know he was going to die?
Yes, he knew. He was convinced he was going to die from the moment he set foot in the hospital.

Is there something that could have saved him?
I'm not sure. Better circumstances maybe? After your mother left and he accepted he had a drinking problem, he sought refuge in his misfortune. I think that was his downfall, and led slowly to the end. He could have asked friends or family for help, but that's easy to say after the fact.

Did he have a happy life?
It's hard to know. I have the impression that your parents had a difficult marriage. I think your father must have felt happy at certain moments of his life, in his work and in the love he felt for his three daughters and his wife, even if maybe he secretly felt like he might care about her more than she cared about him. Overall, I think, sadly, he was unhappy near the end, and I'm sorry that was the case.

I wish you and I could have brought him more happiness. I wish he could have seen how much we love each other, that your work is flourishing and you've found someone you're happy with. It's a bit self-involved to say, but I have the feeling he would have been proud of you, and of the two of us, and maybe that would have made him a little happier too. What do you think? I'm digressing, I know.

/ INTERVIEWEE'S PERSONAL HISTORY

Who are you?
I'm Mario's daughter's boyfriend. Céline's boyfriend. I love Mario's daughter more than anything in the world, except for maybe my mother and my ego.

What is your connection to my father?
Since I didn't get the chance to meet him, my connection is purely imagined, sentimental. I like thinking of him and making up stories. I like thinking he's watching down on us from above—I know, it's a total cliché. Don't tell anyone.

I never got the chance to meet him, but I've crossed paths with him many times in my mind, at random. I shake his hand when we visit; I laugh at his jokes and sometimes get in on them too, just for show, so he'll like me. I like to think our relationship would have been something akin to friendship.

Have you lost a parent? How do you live with that loss?
I'm lucky. I haven't lost anyone close to me yet. I wish things could stay that way forever, but I know that's impossible. Death makes me anxious because it has yet to turn my life upside down. I don't yet know the pain of grieving, but I can imagine what it's like, and it's something I admire about you: that you've known that pain and survived it.

Do you have any comments?
Maybe I'd also have liked for him to be a father figure, a male role model other than my father. If we'd spent time together, we'd have built a strong bond from a sense of family, from shared values and also by our love for you, as different as it is. I think the two of us would have gotten along.

4 of 9

/ PSYCHOLOGICAL PROFILE

Can you tell me, in a few words, who my father was?
I saw a photo of him once. He was handsome. He gave off a kind of masculine energy, like a lot of people from that generation—*soix-ante-huitards*. And he was hairy. That's the impression I got anyway. I might be completely off base… Maybe a little old-school in terms of parenting, he had a hard time managing his daughters' exuberance. Alcohol didn't help him communicate any better. It just fuelled a lot of heated arguments and misunderstandings.

What did you like about him? What were his qualities?
He felt at home in nature, because of his work, and I think you guys also kept rabbits and other animals. That gave him substance, I feel. He carried a knife, for eating and everything else.

Depressed, because he had a drinking problem, and drinking because he was depressed. It's worth thinking about, what it was that crushed our fathers so badly…

He had an addict's relationship to money, wasting it, lacking it, wanting it.

A man broken by the divorce his tired wife asked for.

A man who liked to enjoy life. What kind of music did he listen to?

And his faults?
—

An anecdote?
One time, you snuck out of the house. Your dad found out and waited up for you, drinking, until you got home. When you came back, he was super worked up and chased you around the apartment. You and

your sister jumped out the window and ran away…to an aunt's house maybe? You came home a few days later, because your mom was so upset, I think. It might have been her birthday that day. In any case, you and your sister both went home to make amends. I think after that you were grounded for life!

/ FAMILY HISTORY

Tell me about a few pivotal moments in his life, between his birth and death.
Don't really know.

How did he meet my mother?
I'd love to know the answer to this one…

How did he propose?
She said yes.

What happened after?
They had three pretty daughters.

/ HISTORY OF HIS DEATH

Do you remember what he died of?
Cancer. Maybe because of the pesticides he used at work. Didn't you tell me other people from the farm died of cancer too? But a different kind of cancer, if I remember correctly?

It was almost immediate. He was close to death when he got sick. You couldn't come home before he died; you didn't know it was so serious. Your mother and two sisters were there when you got to the hospital.

Did he know he was going to die?
I can't answer that, since I wasn't nearly close enough. I can only offer half-thoughts that are more questions than anything.

When he'd stop drinking, I imagine he wanted to have hope, even if he relapsed in the end. Maybe in some way, he thought he could get over it; he was still young. Life is full of surprises and hope is part of that. And so is the power of denial.

Is there something that could have saved him?
Save him from what? Sorry, I'm not sure I understand the question.

Did he have a happy life?
It seems like he didn't want to get divorced, and it caused him a lot of pain. He wouldn't be the first.

/ INTERVIEWEE'S PERSONAL HISTORY

Who are you?
A friend.

What is your connection to my father?
When you and I met, he had already died, so I only know what you've told me. I think my memories of our conversations have become muddled with my interpretations and my relationship to my own father. I find our fathers are alike in many ways, not just because of the drinking. Filling this out, I'm a bit mixed up; I don't know anymore if this is something you said to me or if it's what I projected based on my own father–daughter relationship. For example, my dad was very hairy and had a beard back in the day. Did your dad look like that too or did I just imagine him that way?

Anyway, apparently I'm particularly invested in this question- naire.

Have you lost a parent? How do you live with that loss?
—

Do you have any comments?
These weren't easy questions. I feel like a bad friend because I can't remember everything. And there's a lot I want to ask you now. I want to know more, to go back to the seventies and see what he looked like!

5 of 9

/ PSYCHOLOGICAL PROFILE

Can you tell me, in a few words, who my father was?
In a few, yes. But not many more because I didn't know your dad. He clearly had a strong personality. Imposing? He must have had an impact, since you're still following him. And I wonder whether you got that face of yours from him.

What did you like about him? What were his qualities?
—.

And his faults?
—

An anecdote?
—

/ FAMILY HISTORY

Tell me about a few pivotal moments in his life, between his birth and death.
I can't, and it's really too bad. I'm realizing we never talked about his life. You told me about having to rush back to France after he died and that his house was cleared out immediately. Before you had time to take anything. I see that as a pivotal moment. Because it's the only one I know about.

Why do all that? Why put everything in bags and throw it away? Was he all alone? Did he do something wrong? It feels as though it was to erase every trace of him.

How did he meet my mother?

—

How did he propose?

—

What happened after?

—

/ HISTORY OF HIS DEATH

Do you remember what he died of?
I have to admit, I mix up the fathers of my expat friends. Sorry. An
illness, I think, not an accident.

Did he know he was going to die?
We all know. He must have seen it coming if it was, in fact, an illness.
I wonder if he fought. If he had people with him. If he gave up. Did
he want to live?

Is there something that could have saved him?

—

Did he have a happy life?
No. And it's the story about emptying his apartment so quickly that
makes me think not. When someone has a happy life, we want to keep
that person close to us a little longer.

/ INTERVIEWEE'S PERSONAL HISTORY

Who are you?
A friend of Céline's. Emigrated from France to Canada, like her. The
things we know about each other are the things we wanted to bring
with us and, most of all, what we wanted to leave behind.

What is your connection to my father?
Your words, your work. Bits of stories that I mix up with stories of my other friends, as I said.

Have you lost a parent? How do you live with that loss?
No. Grandparents, yes, but that's different, because they were older. And I have a hard time thinking about losing my parents; I'm not ready. Are we ever ready?

A couple years ago, my dad had heart problems. They put in a pacemaker. That's the closest I've come. My first thought was that we still have things to say to each other, that I needed to touch his hands, hear his voice and bury my face in his neck. I'm not ready; I'm afraid of that emptiness.

I'm also afraid of no longer being there for my children. Of them losing me. We can plan for our absence: pay for their studies, limit our debt. I've done all that. But I don't want them to feel the loss of a father, to be left with unanswered questions, for them to do all the things we should have done together with somebody else.

Do you have any comments?
I wondered if I could embellish while filling this out. Invent things. If I knew more about you two, maybe I would have. But I always run away from those discussions. Avoid them, rather. I've never brought it up, out of some sense of propriety, respect, embarrassment, selfishness. It's not easy. We often see each other in a group setting. But I've also never made room for that possibility either. I wonder if you'd even want to talk to me about it. But I guess this questionnaire gives me something of an answer.

6 of 9

/ PSYCHOLOGICAL PROFILE

Can you tell me, in a few words, who my father was?
He was a country man, from a poor family. He married young and
had three daughters before getting divorced. He was a problem-solver
and a hard worker. A farmer. Something of a reactionary. Drinking
wrecked him, and he died too young.

What did you like about him? What were his qualities?
He was a kind of self-taught MacGyver. Bit of a hooligan. He settled
down somewhat after he fell in love with your mom. He knew how to
make you interested in the little things, and he made happy childhood
memories with you.

And his faults?
He didn't understand, or didn't want to understand, the ways others
were different or complex. And he could sometimes be harsh and
narrow-minded because of it, his intolerance coming out in drunken
rages. He could be hurtful and mean. He'd take his unhappiness and
his mistakes out on others. In my opinion, his greatest fault, even if
he couldn't help it, was managing to make you feel guilty for things
that were out of your control.

An anecdote?
I like your childhood memories of him: his little schemes, going fishing, making things—you especially loved that.

/ FAMILY HISTORY

Tell me about a few pivotal moments in his life, between his birth and death.
He grew up in a poor rural area. Lots of kids, his father was a drinker. He didn't get a chance to study and started working young.

How did he meet my mother?
At a Saturday-night dance, the kind where you drink marquisette by the ladle out of a punch bowl and slow-dance up close.

How did he propose?
Clearly asking her went well because they got married.

What happened after?
Kids, crying and baby bottles, happiness, family life, a house, routine, too many drinks at dinner, highs and lows, back-breaking work in the fields, alcohol, divorce, despair and illness.

/ HISTORY OF HIS DEATH

Do you remember what he died of?
He died from the effects of his alcoholism. The drinking had been wreaking havoc on his system for a long time, but the complications suddenly worsened and the end was quick.

Did he know he was going to die?
I don't think he knew it more than at any other moment.

Is there something that could have saved him?
Maybe himself. Michael Jackson's music might have helped.

Did he have a happy life?
Yes, even though I think at some point he lost sight of what happiness was for him, and how to reach it.

/ INTERVIEWEE'S PERSONAL HISTORY

Who are you?
A friend of your father's daughter.

What is your connection to my father?
What I know from you. From what you've told me about him and what I've experienced with or because of him since I've known you.

Have you lost a parent? How do you live with that loss?
My dad is trying to lose me.

Do you have any comments?
You taught me to like your dad despite his faults, his illness and your well-warranted disappointments in him. Thank you for that. He would definitely have liked to know you're happy, in the choices you make and what you do. He would have liked to think he had something to do with it. Whether during or after his time in this world. I think, unlike some people and despite how he acted, your dad loved you and, more than anything, he wanted you to love yourself for who you are.

1

When we arrange them in a different order, photographs, like memories, take on a different meaning.

/

He had stuck a few photos and postcards to the fridge, or maybe to his bedroom door.

7 of 9

/ PSYCHOLOGICAL PROFILE

Can you tell me, in a few words, who my father was?
He was a farmhand. He smoked, he drank and he didn't leave much behind (a photo of himself on a piece of ID, the signature below it).

What did you like about him? What were his qualities?
I like the things you'd tell me sometimes—the tenderness of certain stories.

And his faults?
Can't answer this. I wonder: is it just that you've never told me anything bad about your dad?

An anecdote?
I know that on Saturday mornings, your mom would be tied up with work, and he'd be in the kitchen... He'd make French fries, and for you girls it felt like a special occasion, I think.

/ FAMILY HISTORY

Tell me about a few pivotal moments in his life, between his birth and death.
Can't say.

How did he meet my mother?
All that comes to mind are scenes from that era. And if I think about it, they're stories from my own family. One of my uncles met his future wife at a local dance, another waited outside the office where his girlfriend worked to propose. Memory is faulty: it always leads us back to ourselves.

How did he propose?
No idea…

What happened after?
I'm not sure.

/ HISTORY OF HIS DEATH

Do you remember what he died of?
I drew a blank on this at first, once I finally started filling out the questionnaire. And I felt ashamed (and afraid it would make me seem inattentive, uninterested in a story that is so much a part of you), so I stopped here. Maybe I was more afraid of trying to list an illness (cirrhosis, cancer) and getting it wrong. What I know about him going into the hospital, about his final days, are all things I know from you. Or maybe what I want to say is: I can imagine how acute, how sharp, the pain still is for you. I know you didn't get to see him before he died.

Did he know he was going to die?
I'm not sure.

Is there something that could have saved him?
No, I don't think so.

Did he have a happy life?
In my first, and very rough, draft of the questionnaire, this was the only question I answered. Here is what I initially wrote: "I believe this questionnaire and work to be, in part, an attempt to show that he did— to find evidence of a happy life and, above all, to believe it—without pathos, without the ugliness of condescension."

The last time I modified the file was September 16, 2014. Today, Monday, May 11, 2015, I'm no longer convinced of that answer. My sentence seems too pretty. I don't know anything about your dad's life obviously, but I'm annoyed by what I wrote. We always want to think that when someone dies it's at the end of a happy life. But what if they leave at the end of a sad life, one that's failed in some way, wasted?

/ INTERVIEWEE'S PERSONAL HISTORY

Who are you?
Right now, I'm thirty-three years old. I met you, Céline, in fall 2009 in Montreal. For the first time in a windowless office, then at that gathering in an apartment on Parc Avenue (Halloween maybe?). I teach French at a lycée outside of Paris.

What is your connection to my father?
It's indirect. I met you after he was gone, and then your dad started to take shape little by little, in conversations that were less about getting to know each other and more about mapping out our respective wounds (and of what is off-limits unless we ask first).

Your dad only started to exist for me through your project, out of the interviews with family and people who knew him, and your transcriptions. (I can picture you in a coffee shop on Beaubien, recently back from France, a little MP3 player on the table next to your empty espresso cup.)

Have you lost a parent? How do you live with that loss?
I haven't lost my father or mother, and so far the deaths in our family (a grandmother, an aunt, an uncle and a cousin) have not affected me that much.

Do you have any comments?
I remember a photo: Christelle and Céline, the two oldest, in soccer shorts and jerseys. I'm not sure why but the picture reminds me of him. I can even make out your father somehow, far away, taking the picture of these tall blondes in boys' clothes.

/ PSYCHOLOGICAL PROFILE

Can you tell me, in a few words, who my father was?
I didn't know the man at all. He was Céline's father. He was a young man from a time not too long ago, but a time that seems quite different from our own. He was an agriculturist or farmer, a hard worker. He always had a pocket knife on him. He had three daughters; he adored Céline, the rebel. She was a pain, but that made him proud.

Why do we have kids? So they succeed where we've failed? Does it give us a purpose?

What did you like about him? What were his qualities?
He seemed fun, generous, a bon vivant, rough around the edges but gentle too. If he'd had more space, I'm certain things might have been better. Society broke him, a little like it did Clyde Barrow.

And his faults?
—

An anecdote?
I don't remember what you said exactly, just that your eyes lit up when you told me.

/ FAMILY HISTORY

Tell me about a few pivotal moments in his life, between his birth and death.
He got married really young. Seemingly too young. He was in love with his wife. His love for her seemed different than her feelings for him, even though she did love him back. He looked after his family as best he could, but life never really gave him a break. He had three

girls. Not for a second did he ever think he'd rather have had a boy. He loved life but didn't have time to live it well. He was worn out, and he gave up on his ideals. The bottle never judged, and it lightened the load on his shoulders. But it was a trick, and it killed him in the end.

How did he meet my mother?

—

How did he propose?

—

What happened after?

—

/ HISTORY OF HIS DEATH

Do you remember what he died of?
He died because of life. It didn't happen the way Céline wanted, but maybe it was the way he would have wanted.

Did he know he was going to die?
Yes. In some cases, it can seem strange to go before you've taken the time to say your goodbyes. But I find that, most times, saying goodbye can hurt more.

Is there something that could have saved him?
Isn't it religion that invented the verb for "salvation"?

Did he have a happy life?
What does that mean, a happy life? I don't know what your father's criteria were for a happy life.

/ INTERVIEWEE'S PERSONAL HISTORY

Who are you?
Defining myself in two sentences would be completely reductive. But okay, I'll bite. I was raised to be a girl, and I've spent my life trying to understand what that means.

What is your connection to my father?
Your dad was the man who was your father. My connection to him is you.

Have you lost a parent? How do you live with that loss?
—

Do you have any comments?
I can't get over the fact that I cried while filling this out.

9 of 9

/ PSYCHOLOGICAL PROFILE

Can you tell me, in a few words, who my father was?
I imagine him looking like you. So: tall.

I imagine a Frenchman. With Nordic origins. Maybe Danish. Flemish? Dutch? You told me, but I can't remember. He might have had light-coloured eyes.

A handsome man.

What did you like about him? What were his qualities?
He was a nice man. I imagine him that way because he's your dad. I would have a hard time imagining him otherwise. Nice, but complicated. Someone who hasn't led an unhappy life but didn't have the life he wanted.

And his faults?
A man who's perhaps a bit tortured. Overly sensitive.

An anecdote?
That woman he loved when he was young... Where is she? Who is she?

/ FAMILY HISTORY

Tell me about a few pivotal moments in his life, between his birth and death.
He had three daughters. All very different. He raised them, as a father raises daughters.

How did he meet my mother?
Very young. Maybe too young. After romantic disappointment. A love lost forever. He met your mother—another love, a profound one.

How did he propose?
I'm against marriage, so I'm skipping this question.

What happened after?
They lived happily ever after and had three daughters.
They lived as best they could and had three daughters.
They lived relatively happily and had three daughters.
And then he died.

/ HISTORY OF HIS DEATH

Do you remember what he died of?
He died of an illness. Cancer, I think. A long, horrible illness, for him and you and your sisters. It's hard to watch someone who's sick and suffering, and not be able to do anything about it.

Did he know he was going to die?
Yes. I think he knew. But that he didn't want to die, he wasn't ready. Not just because he was too young, but because as death draws closer, few people, even when they're suffering a great deal, very few people are ready to die or want to die. So he knew but he didn't want to.
Or was it an accident?

Is there something that could have saved him?
—

Did he have a happy life?
I don't know. I'm worried the answer might be no. And that it's the answer you're looking for in writing this book.

/ INTERVIEWEE'S PERSONAL HISTORY·

Who are you?
I'm someone you don't know very well, and who didn't know your dad
or the relationship you had with him.

What is your connection to my father?
You're the only connection I have to your dad. What you've told me—
the bits and pieces—is always in connection with your book. And I
didn't venture to ask questions, even though I wanted to. So I've had
to make things up.

Have you lost a parent? How do you live with that loss?
I've lost all my grandparents. I have memories of spending time in
the country with them. Stills, like photos imprinted onto my brain.
My maternal grandmother died first, when I was seven. I didn't really
know what death was. I learned by watching others grieve.

Then my grandfather died when I was nine. I didn't go to either of
their funerals. I still think about them, about the fact that my mother
has been an orphan for thirty years now. And sometimes I tell myself
they're watching me or can see me from wherever they are (leftovers
from Catechism, I guess).

I lost my dad nine years ago, the year I turned twenty. He was tall,
he had light-coloured eyes. He was perfectly imperfect. He died after
a long illness. He was old. And I saw how, little by little, he got calmer,
maybe from a sort of wisdom that came with age, and a certainty that
the end was near. He became even more loving. Then he died.

He was older than all my friends' fathers; I remember thinking of
him dying and imagining it would be when I was still young. I didn't
find his death unfair. I cried a lot and sometimes I still do. I'm scared
that I'll end up forgetting him. I was there when he died. It was one of
the most beautiful and radiant moments I've lived. That's something
I don't often say out loud, because it sounds strange. But the final

moments, his breath slowing, until it was gone—that was the most terrible and painful experience of my life; I don't usually want to think a lot about those last moments.

Do you have any comments?
I don't want to be an orphan.

/

Philippe told me that a woman named Annick Tanne loved my father very much. I scribbled her name on a scrap of paper and slipped it into my pocket.

Scene 5

CÉLINE, THE MOTHER

The mother is lying on a sofa, her legs stretched out. It's evening, maybe night. She can't sleep. A reading lamp illuminates the pages she's determined to read to forget how restless she is. She scans them quickly, as though reviewing a contract under the watch of some salesperson or banker.

She writes short replies in the blank spaces Céline has left for her.

CÉLINE: What's your connection to Papa?

THE MOTHER: *(Writing in pencil)* His wife.

CÉLINE: How did you two meet?

THE MOTHER: At a local dance.

CÉLINE: What was it that you liked about him?

THE MOTHER: *(On two lines)* I was insecure. I needed someone to take an interest in me.

CÉLINE: Was he the one who asked you to marry him? How did you end up getting engaged?

THE MOTHER: We talked it over together.

CÉLINE: How did you feel when he died?

THE MOTHER: Very sad. I wanted him to pull through for the sake of you three. You still needed a dad. We lived together for twenty-six years. We *[redacted]*. Even though life together was hard, I loved him, and I wanted so badly for him to change.

CÉLINE: Can you tell me how you found out he died?

THE MOTHER: We were in Brittany. Christelle called. I remember we'd been at Yann's mother's for lunch that day. We packed our bags and came home.

CÉLINE: Do you think he knew he was going to die?

THE MOTHER: I can't say. I didn't see him anymore by that point.

Scene 6

THE MOTHER, CÉLINE

They're in the living room, the mother sitting on the sofa, the daughter across from her in the armchair. The audio recorder rests on the table. They had planned to discuss a husband and a father, but talking about him led them to all sorts of things the mother had buried deep down so she wouldn't fall apart. At one point, when Céline brings up her experience in psychotherapy, her mother says, "That would have killed me."

But instead she's in pain. She's been in pain for years. Her back, mostly. She used to tower over everyone and now her daughters stand taller. Her lumbar discs are compressed. But the worst, she says, is her legs. The discs crush the nerves in her spine, and her legs burn and itch constantly, or they spasm all night while she's sleeping. The doctors just keep changing her prescription, telling her she's too sensitive—or unhappy maybe? And Céline thinks of her grandmother, whom she barely knew.

THE MOTHER: I've got nothing on my mother.

CÉLINE: She has Alzheimer's, right?

THE MOTHER: No, I don't think so. It's not Alzheimer's. It's just that she has no one left. The only people she sees are doctors. It's making her crazy. She's still her same old moody self.

CÉLINE: You saw her again?

THE MOTHER: Yes, and I'm glad I did, because there were questions I wanted to ask her and I got to ask them.

CÉLINE: How did that go?

THE MOTHER: She didn't answer straight away. Then that night, she lost it and called me a… It was horrible. But I stood up to her for the first time ever. I stood up to her and asked for an explanation. But she couldn't give me one. She just said, "Doesn't your mind ever get completely muddled?" And I said, "No, Mom, never to that extent." I spent a few days with her. When we had the fight, I took my phone and went for a walk. I called Yann; he was worried about me. I went back once I'd calmed down. It's really hard, you know, when you… when you're staying with someone and you have a fight. Because you have to go back there. Nothing happened after that though. We went to bed, and the next day things were a tiny bit better. I cleaned her bathroom just for something to do. She said, "Oh, that's nice of you. It hasn't been this clean in ages." And then after, "Okay, give it a rest with the bathroom."

CÉLINE: And that was it?

THE MOTHER: No. When she drove me to the train station, she said, "Thank you for being so kind. I'm sorry for all the rotten stuff I've put you through."

CÉLINE: So you never got answers to your questions?

THE MOTHER: What are you going to do. It is what it is.

CÉLINE: Still, it must have changed something that you were able to stand up to her.

THE MOTHER: Yes, exactly. I asked her why she didn't raise me. Why she sent me to live with my grandmother. She didn't know what to say. And I asked why she hadn't wanted anything to do with the three of you either. I called her when you were born. And I have no idea how many calls it took before she came. She didn't even hold you, or look at you. She told me she was moving down to Bandol.

Pause.

CÉLINE: And then?

THE MOTHER: Then she asked me why we hadn't seen each other for ten years.

CÉLINE: Did you tell her?

THE MOTHER: I told her. I said, "I was busy raising my kids. And I had Dad and Marc to look after." Marc was still little when she left.

CÉLINE: What did she say?

THE MOTHER: Nothing. She realized it was a good reason.

CÉLINE: Was she loving with your brothers and sisters?

THE MOTHER: She wasn't loving with anyone.

Long pause. They look at one another.

When she learned of her grandmother's death, Céline did not go back to France. Her grandmother had thrown herself from her bedroom window in the retirement home where she lived. On the note she left behind, she'd written, "Tell my children I'm sorry, but I just can't bear these legs anymore."

DREAMS

May 2004

I see my father through the window of the airplane, flying in my direction, his arms wide open, until he's so close his face is pressed against the glass.

October 2004

My sister is piling on the guilt. "We all know how unreliable you are." She says I'm mean too. "Papa thought the same thing. You're mean and you're irresponsible." I can't even defend myself since she's quoting my dead father. In the family hierarchy, the oldest sister is the keeper of the family story, so what she says about my father can only be true: she would know.

I need to find a way to protect myself against these accusations though. I try to push the words out of my throat. In the dream, my words are tiny objects, and speaking means forcing them up through my trachea. It makes me feel like throwing up, and I do, surprised at how easily my body goes from nausea to vomiting, as though all I had to do was think of something in order for it to happen.

December 2004

My father is sitting at the table, arms crossed, and he's covered in bandages up to his eyes. A volley of sentences goes through my mind when I look at him: I feel bad for him, I love him, he's my dad, he's harmless. When I open my mouth to tell him what I didn't have time to say while he was alive, the bandages fall from his face and it's no longer my father. There is no one at all.

June 2006

As a child I often dreamed I was alone in the house. In the dream, I hear the familiar sound of my father's car pulling in. I go outside to meet him. It's dark. I hear an axe striking wood, as I often do in the evenings when we need to light a fire in the fireplace. It's always winter in the dream. I call out, "Papa, is that you?" No answer. I walk along the edge of the house until I reach the corner, then I see an axe rise above my head. I remembered the dream this morning, after being woken from a different dream.

July 2008

I'm hugging my dad tightly, and I tell him something I've never told him before. He asks me to repeat it so he'll know it's true. I scream it with all my might, so loudly that it pulls me from my dream. Then a heavy sadness sets in as I realize I still haven't been able to tell my father what I thought I'd told him that night in the dream, because he's no longer alive.

October 2010

My ex-boyfriend Patrick comes to visit me at my father's. My father calls him a bastard under his breath, which I find embarrassing, but more embarrassing still is that my father has seen me with this man (this asshole, as he called him). My father hates him after hearing the story of an abortion, a story he still can't fathom.

A car slows down near the fence in our yard. A child is sitting in the back seat. I walk over, waiting for the driver to roll down the windows, and I ask the little girl her name. I'm not sure why, but I can tell by her answer that she belongs to them: Patrick and the woman driving. Then Patrick, who's worried I might make a scene, quips in his own defence, "It's just that, with her, I don't need to use complicated words anymore!" I don't answer. I go back in the house and leave Patrick alone on the street. He leans against the fence and stares at me staring at him through the living room window. Mortified, I realize my father must have heard the whole thing.

October 2010
I am living in Tokyo in a skyscraper with my mother and one of my sisters. A storm is shaking the foundation, rocking the building from side to side, harder and harder. Water surrounds us. Giant waves form in the distance and crash into the tower, which cracks, like the ruined tower I always pull from my tarot deck, and I tell my mom and my sister we'll need to jump to make it out alive. Then I jump. I motion to them from below, and they look down at me through the bay window of our beautiful loft. But they don't jump. They just keep living in the broken tower, which in the end doesn't crumble. I find myself in a slum where I live on the roof of a house with other so-called illegals. There isn't much room: each of us has a space the size of a yoga mat. I have to wait till nightfall to scale the wall without being seen and reach my small patch of roof. It's a hard life. A man's life, of men as bearded and penniless as my father.

December 2010
My sister tells me my father is dead. The news hurts. Maybe even more than the first time. I tell my roommate I have to go to France because they're throwing out all his things, everything he owns.

December 2010
My aunt and uncle arrive at a family party. They've learned that I'd like

to interview them about my father, and they want to do the interview right away. I'm somewhat caught off guard, and I can't find my Dictaphone. I'm worried I'm taking too long and they might change their minds, so I decide just to use my phone. François is holding a piece of paper with sentences written out in two columns. Parts of the page are blank and much of it is crossed out. My father comes into the room and wants to know what the hell we're doing. I don't dare tell him we're writing about his death.

July 2011

I'd quit my job and stolen a locomotive. I was with my roommate, Geneviève. We'd just put in an offer for a new house; I knew they, whoever they are, might find out because of this, since my father's name would be written in our application, but I said nothing. I guess I didn't want to deprive Geneviève of the joy of a new home.

A girl came running out of a hangar toward me. She wanted to warn me that they'd found me. I didn't try to get away. During the trial—there was a trial—my lawyers didn't think it was possible I'd get life in prison for such minor infractions, but I did. I might have even been sentenced to death, I'm not sure anymore. Before being sent to prison, everyone watches a video in which Martin says he's going to end his life soon. It's the end of an era, and I find it sad. Geneviève can't believe it.

July 2011

My father is sick. He's in the bathroom throwing up blood, and my grandmother is looking after him. She seems very worried. My father is emaciated. His cheeks are hollow and his eyes are bulging. "Can't you see he's going to die?" I yell. No one hears me. I'm standing behind a pane of glass, like a detective behind an interrogation-room window. My father's wearing striped pyjamas, like in movies about Auschwitz.

August 2011

I find my father healthy, glowing, eyes shining. "Nothing like your passport photo," I say.

March 2012

My father is scaling the front of the house, and I have to yell for him to hear me. He slips under a balcony railing and disappears. I ask a question and he doesn't answer. I yell, "Why don't you answer me?" Then, "Papa, answer me! Answer me!" There's someone with me and she enters the house and goes upstairs. She realizes my father can't answer because he's been electrocuted by the wires strewn across the floor. He's lying on the ground, unconscious, perhaps already dead. I call my mother: "Mom, Mom! Mom, call an ambulance!" She comes into the room and leans over him to take his pulse. The person with us stops her, so that she doesn't get electrocuted when she touches him.

May 2012

My mother comes into my room. She starts going through my stuff, telling me she's sure some possession of mine has been stolen. She empties my drawers and shelves and asks if I know what is missing. "Is it this? Did someone steal this? Or this?"

My father is giving a performance and we're in the audience. I step up onto the stage to act in a scene, but it happens differently this time. I realize there are multiple versions of the scene, and I've never noticed before tonight, because I've never stayed until the end of the play.

May 2012

My father sits in the kitchen, resting his elbows on a Formica table I thought we'd gotten rid of ages ago. Every item of furniture in the house is something we threw away. The air smells like dust.

May 2012

I've just moved into a big house with Geneviève. It has an infinite number of rooms. I live in the right half of the house and she lives in the left. The house is so huge that we can sleep in a different room every night, so I switch to a bigger bedroom with its own bathroom at the end of a long corridor. Martin tells me not to—someone got sick in that room. I know he's right but I move my stuff in anyway, without disinfecting anything. The house hides something else too: a secret, a body in the basement, perhaps my father's. In the end, I'm convinced the house can bring us no good and we should leave as soon as we can.

September 2012

Someone has killed themselves, and it's kind of my fault. I get ready to leave, gathering my things and placing them in a small paper bag. I tell myself that this person's death might not be entirely irreversible yet, and I don't know what to do anymore, whether to stay and save them or to leave and save myself.

September 2012

My father has tried to commit suicide. It's not his first attempt, but no one has mentioned the other times to me. In my dream, I think, *I'd rather have a suicidal father than a dead one.*

November 2012

My mother and I are in a car. We drive past my father's farm. I cry out, "Oh! Let's stop." I'm anxious to get out because I have my camera with me, and I want to take photos of what I think of as my father's places. But my camera is stuck on a macro-function that takes extreme close-ups even though I want long shots. I look at the beautiful landscapes I can't capture because my camera won't work properly.

April 2013

This morning, my father is looking after me. He pours my cereal and I say to him that he must be happy to be a father. Just before this, my mother made me cry when she asked me to stop letting my T-shirts mould in my father's workshop sink. I was hurt that she could think that of me, that I was the one who did it. I haven't even set foot in there in a year. "Your father's the one who said it was you." I cried harder, knowing he'd accused me. He apologized straight away—he must have been mistaken.

November 2013

I have an iguana wrapped around my neck. I have to be careful that nothing catches its skin, or the skin will rip. I wonder if it's my skin, this iguana or the memory of my father that's choking me and that I'm protecting from the worst kind of harm: being forgotten.

March 2014

My father starts yelling loudly at my mother. He looks half-crazed, different from a second ago, when he was acting entirely normal. I step in and scream at him to stop. I grab his arm, the one he hits my mother with. For a second, I have the impression I could break his arm like you'd break a dry branch, by snapping it in two against my thigh with both hands. The thought frightens me, and I let go.

At that moment, I see my father standing behind the glass living-room door. He's holding my little cousin's arm and threatening to break it the same way I imagined breaking his. Then, in his hand, it's a bit of wood he snaps, and not an arm.

My sister comes home. My mother grabs my father's arm and quickly hides it behind her back, so as not to upset my sister. She hates it when they fight.

February 2015

I'm investigating my father's death and I keep getting threats. My car gets broken into. My apartment gets robbed and all my notebooks stolen. I make my roommate change the locks. "To make sure it doesn't happen again," I tell him. "Don't give anyone the keys. I'll give one key to…another to…, one to the landlord and to…" I give him an endless list of people to whom I'll give our keys.

April 2015
I had two dreams about my father. In the first, he died before I could see him again. It was devastating. In the second, I didn't remember anymore, but I thought it must hurt to lose a father twice.

June 2015
We're headed to my father's gravesite and I can't stop crying. At times, I realize I don't really want to cry anymore but I cry nonetheless, like when you're making love to someone and you keep moaning long after you're no longer turned on.

September 2015
To prepare a section of the book about my father, I go to a shooting range and rent a fancy new rifle that fires in bursts. I have trouble aiming. And then I realize I forgot to bring the photos with me that I wanted to use, so I cut out magazine pictures of perfect women to use instead. I attach one of the women to the barrel of the gun and, when I fire, she's propelled onto the cardboard target at the end of the firing lane. I'm extremely proud of my creative process.

The man who runs the shooting range tells us he hasn't had sexual relations since his wife's throat was slit while he was taking her from behind. That's what he says. "That's not the kind of thing you forget."

September 2015
I had a dream last night, about my father. I know because I woke up laughing and I told myself, I need to write it down so I can put it in my book.

DIALOGUES—III

Scene 7

CÉLINE, THE MOTHER, CHRISTELLE

In the mother's living room, during the first interview. She and Céline are alone.

CÉLINE: I'd like to know about his childhood. Where he was born, where he grew up…

THE MOTHER: He was born in Saint-Germain-de-la-Grange— Wait, what am I saying? He was born in Chantepie. When you drive out of Plaisir, you head toward Chavenay. There are one or two houses in the fields, on the left. That's where he was born.

CÉLINE: He was born at the house?

THE MOTHER: They all were, the whole family. You knew that he lost his mom when he was five or six?

CÉLINE: Did he ever talk to you about it?

THE MOTHER: He didn't really remember much about her. So he never talked about it, no.

CÉLINE: So it was pretty much Jeanne who raised him?

THE MOTHER: Not really. Jeanne already had kids of her own. Not the younger three yet, but she had Francis when she was fourteen, then Noëlle and Michel. She didn't really have time to look after her brothers. Mario grew up without a mom. You could tell it had affected him. *(She mumbles.)* You could tell it had been hard on him.

CÉLINE: He was on his own, then.

THE MOTHER: Pretty much. And everyone was always at each other's throats in that house. They didn't hit each other, but they got close. There was a lot of drinking too. They didn't really have money for food, but there was alcohol. There was always alcohol in the house. Jeanne once said to me, "When I first met you, I thought you were a real bore, because you didn't like to drink."

CHRISTELLE: That all happened before I was born, so I don't know. So maybe it's true they fought all the time. But family has always been really important to Papa. And friends.

CÉLINE: Everyone drank?

THE MOTHER: For them, it's a religion. A religion. Patrice was probably the one who drank the least.

CÉLINE: Oh really? Patrice… He's the one who died in a car crash?

110

THE MOTHER: In Portugal. He was divorced. Some of the people he worked with were Portuguese, and they invited him there on vacation. Patrice brought his son with him. The car fell into a ravine.

CÉLINE: I didn't know Patrice, but I always got the impression he was different. It's the feeling I get looking at the photographs.

THE MOTHER: He was a really wonderful person. He was the oldest. When your grandparents had him, they weren't married yet, so Patrice had his mother's name: Lessage. Marcel, your grandpa, never bothered doing the paperwork to change it. When he got called up for military service, they used his legal name, Patrice Lessage, and from then on everyone hated him.

Céline pictures the scene: a gendarme coming to get Patrice to force him to do his "three days"—his military service. The boys pushed things too far, jeering at their brother, calling him a bastard. And enraging their father. The scene ends, but the shame does not. A shame that, unconsciously, feeds the boys' daily anger against their brother. Bastard, implying an illegitimacy that clearly takes aim at the mother: unbearable because it makes imaginable a woman's infidelity.

THE MOTHER: Personally, I liked him a lot. Your dad didn't really get along with him. When I first started dating your dad, Patrice invited us for dinner. We had a drink, and I don't remember what your dad said, something like, "You're a Lessage." Things got heated, and we had to leave. And yet they both had the same mother. But anyway, I didn't bother trying—

CÉLINE: To understand?

THE MOTHER: To understand. Your father wasn't exactly easy either. He could be stubborn. When you tried to talk to him, he'd get his back up. End of discussion.

CÉLINE: He wasn't good at talking about how he felt?

THE MOTHER: He acted like he was being skinned alive. What I always said was: I know you had an unhappy childhood, and I understand, but you have a great life now—the girls are great, you have a house, you have a job, try to see the positive side of things.

CÉLINE: And he couldn't?

THE MOTHER: Nothing to be done.

CÉLINE: When I was little, I remember you talking about an illegitimate child. That was Patrice?

THE MOTHER: Ah no, there was another one. When Marcel was younger, he worked on a farm. Because, you see, your grandfather was a ward of the state. He worked on a farm and he slept with a girl on the farm, and she had a kid…

CÉLINE: But he never acknowledged he was the father?

THE MOTHER: No, no.

CÉLINE: Did Papa know him?

THE MOTHER: He knew him to see him.

CÉLINE: But they never spoke?

THE MOTHER: No.

CÉLINE: And the boy, did he know who his father was?

THE MOTHER: Yes, he knew.

CÉLINE: And what about the mother?

THE MOTHER: We used to go out to eat in Crespières sometimes. I wonder if she wasn't one of the two women who owned the restaurant we'd go to. It wasn't any of my business; I didn't want to get involved.

CÉLINE: Papa never talked to you about it?

THE MOTHER: No. And in any case, it was his father's problem, not his. The mother apparently raised the kid on her own, and that's it.

/

As a girl, I had fallen in love with Mario, but I could have fallen in love with anyone: a body to which we end up attributing who knows what meanings. ... you don't know who he really is, he doesn't know himself.
—Elena Ferrante, *The Days of Abandonment*
(tr. Ann Goldstein)

Scene 8

PHILIPPE, CÉLINE, MARC, ANNETTE

Céline is alone with Philippe in her mother's apartment. They sit down on the sofas, facing each other.

PHILIPPE: Everyone loved him. He was the family favourite. In your mom and Annette's family too. I was the bad kid. Your grandfather never trusted me. Not sure why. Even your mom didn't want to talk to me for a stretch. But your dad, everyone loved him.

CÉLINE: When did you two meet?

PHILIPPE: We grew up together. He lived next door. We'd tell people we were cousins. No one blinked an eye. *(He thinks back.)* Your grandfather worked with my dad a lot.

CÉLINE: They were bricklayers?

PHILIPPE: Cement masons. They knew how to make concrete. Your dad and I were at school together. *(Laughs)* Played hooky together, more like. We'd sneak into student parties on the weekends. The booze was half the price. Those were wild nights. You should have seen the two of us. Saturdays we'd drink a case of beer, then take our mopeds and go to the dance.

Mario liked to tell the story about how he built his moped from an old chassis. Brakes, wheels, transmission—every night he'd strip the parts he needed off the mopeds parked along the street, one by one, then use them to build his own.

PHILIPPE: He was going out with your mom, and I was seeing Annette. My brother had gone out with her before. But not for long.

He tells Céline about the pool where the four of them used to swim. They called it a pool, but it was more of a pond. Céline pictures her mom at twenty—sensible, a little shy, embarrassed but won over by the two men and their shameless ways. She was probably still studying biochemistry. Or else she was done school and looking for work. She was two years older than Mario.

PHILIPPE: After we dropped out of school, we worked together for the blacksmith. We made tools for the Bridges and Roads Corps—must have been a hundred degrees in there. *(He shows the burn scars on his hands.)* His brother got us the job.

CÉLINE: Patrice? And they got along?

PHILIPPE: They were close. Never fought. *(He lights a cigarette.)* Often we'd go straight to the shop after a night out. Your dad showed up for work no matter what. Patrice would have killed him otherwise. I'd sneak a nap behind a tree or something. With the heat and the smell, your dad would be out before long to throw up all the booze. Patrice would shake his head and say, "I won't even ask where the other one is."

MARC: He was always passionate about what he did.

PHILIPPE: Later the smithy got bought up by some engineers. They drove us nuts with all their calculations. We'd have to heat something for this long, cool it for that long. I was the first to clear out. Then your dad. Then Patrice.

ANNETTE: Your parents lived with the Forget family. It was their first apartment after they got married and Christelle was born.

PHILIPPE: He lived with the Forgets. You won't be able to get anything from them about your dad. They had a falling-out. Your dad left and they never spoke again. In any case, the old man is dead.

MARC: After, he worked with his brother Gaëtan, pouring concrete. He didn't like it. He stayed a year and a half, around the time Christelle was born. And he started working on the farm in seventy-seven. He was twenty.

PHILIPPE: Hervé was the one who gave him that first farm job. And Hervé sold him the first house you lived in. Mario was already renting the place from him for cheap. Then he bought it. Hervé let him pay it off in installments. That helped—that and the farm work. *(He looks at Céline.)* Hervé's dead now too.

Scene 9

ÉLODIE, CÉLINE, CHRISTELLE, PHILIPPE, THE MOTHER

From here on, it's no longer clear when or in which house the lines are spoken.

ÉLODIE: I loved visiting the farm. Do you remember when we'd go sledding on the grain heap?

CÉLINE: Papa wasn't happy when he saw us. Was it because there were rats in the shed?

ÉLODIE: No. It was because we scattered grain all over the place. He was worried his boss would be mad if he saw. But I think he couldn't help but laugh when he saw us going down the hill of corn on our asses. A few years later, the grain wasn't kept in the shed anymore, it went straight to the silos.

CÉLINE: Did you get the feeling Papa was happy at the farm?

CHRISTELLE: When he was working there, you mean?

CÉLINE: Yeah.

CHRISTELLE: I think he liked his job. But it isn't like he could have done anything else, because he really needed to...

CÉLINE AND CHRISTELLE: ...be outside.

They laugh at saying this at the same time.

PHILIPPE: The folks on the farm were a kind of second family. Perrochon, the boss, was like a father to him. When Perrochon's daughter took over the farm and let your dad go, it was a blow. He tried another two or three jobs, but nothing stuck.

CÉLINE: Do you know if he would have liked to do something different with his life?

THE MOTHER: *(Pausing)* No, he found what he—

CHRISTELLE: Drawing. That was his big regret. He used to tell me all the time how he'd studied industrial design, but that he had to quit, because of the money. He must have brought that up a hundred times.

CÉLINE: He said his teacher had been impressed to see him drafting freehand. But he had to stop because he didn't have the money for supplies. After that, he signed up for a sewing class. It was a great way to pick up girls, since he was the only guy in the class. I always thought that's where he met mom.

THE MOTHER: I don't know if he wanted to do anything else. You know, your dad never talked about what he wanted. He'd had to fend for himself since he was a kid. His dad didn't look after him. Jeanne had her own kids, so she couldn't help. If he didn't want to go to school, he just didn't go. He was on the verge of going down a bad road. He used to steal records. He used to steal a lot of things.

CÉLINE: What straightened him out?

THE MOTHER: Well, he met me.

CÉLINE: So it was you?

THE MOTHER: You better believe it.

Scene 10

A NEIGHBOUR, ANNETTE, MARC, THE MOTHER, CÉLINE,
A FRIEND OF CÉLINE'S, CHRISTELLE, ANOTHER NEIGH-
BOUR, PHILIPPE

A NEIGHBOUR: Your dad was a real character. Got up to a lot of mischief. You should ask Marc about that. They spent a lot of time together.

ANNETTE: I don't know that he got up to a lot of mischief. Not really. The police were never involved, in any case. He was a cool guy. A nice guy. We all used to go dancing—your father, your mom, Philippe and me. He was always kind and generous.

MARC: Once we went back to Annette's, and there was all this construction material lying around on the building site next to her place. We brought your mom home and then we went back and loaded up the car. Your dad suggested we take the side streets, to avoid the cops. Just our luck: we hit a pothole and the car was so heavy we blew a tire. We started unloading the stolen material into a field. First car that went by was a cop car. They told us to follow them to the station. We got home around six the next morning.

THE MOTHER: I'd been waiting for them since midnight.

CÉLINE: *(To Marc)* You'd go dancing with them?

MARC: *(Hesitating)* Yeah, I'd go dancing...

THE MOTHER: Of course you didn't. You were too young! The four of us used go, by moped: Annette, Philippe, Mario and me.

Céline asks everyone she interviews the same question:

CÉLINE: Do you remember any one thing in particular about Papa?

A NEIGHBOUR: When there was a funeral, he never wanted to go into the church. He'd wait out front with his dog. That was his excuse. He said he wouldn't set foot in the Lord's house so long as beasts weren't allowed in. It drove your mother crazy.

ANNETTE: He used to say, "The farther away God is, the better off I am." He always had a joke for everything.

MARC: Once he trimmed the hedges for a client of the farm, and she gave him a 1966 Margaux to thank him. We drank it with your mom—a decent bottle, if you like apple cider.

Marc bursts out laughing. He adds that they drank the bottle even though it was corked, he and Mario and Christiane (that's the mother's name). Then he stops talking for a second to think. His face lights up.

MARC: Ah, and fishing! He loved to fish! I'm sure I've got tons of fishing stories.

CÉLINE: That summer when he took me night fishing with him in the port of Saint-Gilles-Croix-de-Vie, I was really proud. There were hardly any patrols at night so we could try to go without a licence. We'd sit side by side and wait for a bite. Papa would let me use his cloth folding stool.

One night, a fishing boat passing too close to the dock caught Céline's line before she had time to reel it in. Without missing a beat, the father cut the fishing line at the end of the pole with his pocket knife. The reel, whirling fast, stopped immediately. Céline held tight to the pole, deter-

mined to hang on to it at whatever cost. Another time, Céline reeled in a massive eel, without really intending to, and her father told the family the story for ages afterward. She was so proud. His recognition wasn't easy to earn. You had to be remarkable. And the requirements differed for the oldest, the youngest and the middle child—good at school, pretty, funny, a vivid imagination, excellent manners.

A FRIEND OF CÉLINE'S: He was incredibly kind and generous. He was crazy about you and your sisters. That much was clear. Sure, he was awkward: he didn't know how to show people affection. But he did everything he could to make sure you wanted for nothing. That was his way.

THE MOTHER: What I remember is how, once he settled in somewhere with his fishing rod, you couldn't get him to leave. If it was raining, I'd wait in the car with you girls. I'd say, "We've got the kids with us." And he'd grumble and tell me to go home, that he'd find his own way back.

MARC: Fishing was a bit of a drag for me too. He could stay there for days, just sitting there, whatever the weather. But what I did love was going mushroom picking with him. He knew all the different species of mushrooms and all the best spots. He knew a lot of things.

CHRISTELLE: Papa was good at making things. He could make anything from almost nothing. He taught us how to whistle with a blade of grass between our thumbs. He made us flutes out of bamboo sticks and cigarette paper. He climbed a tree to put up a swing for us. He made us dream, and he made us laugh when his projects failed. Like the time he wanted to teach us how to take the shell of a hard-boiled egg off in one piece, by piercing a little hole at each end. But just his luck, he hadn't let the egg boil long enough. He blew into the hole and runny egg shot out onto the wall.

MARC: One time we went out to cut wood and we almost got crushed under a tree. Normally when you fell a tree, you make a notch into the side you want the tree to fall on. Then you make your way around the tree and do the other side with the chainsaw. But when it was about to fall, the tree twisted, because of the knots, and came down on us. It was a big, bushy tree. Your dad made sure I was safe before he ran out of the way. That's how he was.

A NEIGHBOUR: He was immensely knowledgeable. He taught me how to plot out my garden to grow the most food and not leach the earth or use fertilizer. He knew a lot about animals too. He couldn't stand seeing them harmed. Once I put out traps in my garden because a dog had eaten our chickens during the waxing moon. Your dad wasn't happy. He sure gave me a piece of his mind.

CÉLINE: Every spring he'd clean the gutters. He'd throw out the dead leaves and clear out the sparrow nests. He'd lean over, standing on the ladder, and pick up the baby birds one by one and dangle them over the dog, who'd be growling with delight, then drop them. I'd shout so loud at each bird getting gobbled up by the dog that eventually he'd give me one. We'd put it in a shoe filled with cotton batting. The baby birds looked like bats. They usually died during the night.

A NEIGHBOUR: He had a big heart too, your dad.

A FRIEND OF CÉLINE'S: I remember something that's not that interesting in and of itself. But it sums up who your dad is, in my mind. One time my car broke down outside Bazoches. I called your dad, and half an hour later he was there. I remember thanking him over and over for coming, and he turned to me and said, "You're like a daughter; of course I came." My dad had just left my mom, and she was sleeping all the time. I'd completely lost my bearings, and he could tell. His words really anchored me. I've never forgotten that.

PHILIPPE: One time we were walking and I saw flowers in a greenhouse. I said, "Hey, I'll grab some for your wife." "Quit fooling around," he told me. But I did it anyways. It was just before he married your mom. When I went in, the lights came on. We booted it out of there, but the village constable caught up with us. He whacked me in the stomach with the end of a pickaxe and knocked me to the ground. When your dad realized I wasn't behind him, he doubled back and decked the guy. If you messed with me, you messed with him, and vice versa. It was the same at dances. If you fought one of us, you fought both of us.

CÉLINE: *(To her mother)* Do you remember that?

THE MOTHER: No, I don't think so.

MARC: Philippe was always one to stretch the truth. The two of us never got along.

A NEIGHBOUR: Your dad liked following leaders. He liked putting himself behind them, never in front.

MARC: When he told stories, he was never the hero. He always made room for everyone else. That's why I liked being around him.

A NEIGHBOUR: The people he chose to love, the people he shared things with, he loved them body and soul.

CÉLINE: He never said it, but he showed it. He gave a lot of gifts.

CHRISTELLE: Gifts were his way of… I don't think he'd gotten much love. Growing up, expressing emotions just wasn't something any of them did. Same for Mom's side of the family.

Scene 11

THE MOTHER: When I had Christelle, I only saw your father for an hour.

CÉLINE: He didn't go with you to the hospital?

THE MOTHER: He didn't have his driver's licence, so my mom was the one who drove me. He'd been at the fairgrounds all weekend, and he fell asleep on the grass in front of the hospital. My dad woke him up by dumping a bucket of water over his head. *(She laughs, despite the pain this memory stirs up.)* When he came into the hospital room to visit me, he was still drunk.

MARC: We went out for a drink to celebrate the new baby—me, your dad and Philippe. We met these three guys who loaded us into their Citroën 2CV to take us to another bar. By the time we got there, we were hammered. We were joking around, saying, "You shouldn't have jacked that car." It was just a joke, but someone must have heard us and called the cops, because they picked us up as we were leaving. The guys didn't have a car key. They'd twist or untwist the contact wires to stop and start the engine. The cops grilled us all night, and the next day too. Finally they let us go. Your dad went straight to the hospital. He was so exhausted that he fell asleep on the lawn. Dad came and woke him up with a bucket of water. I went home to sleep.

CÉLINE: Did it make you sad?

THE MOTHER: Well, yes. I didn't ask a lot, but there were things I needed and didn't get. He was never very affectionate. He never held me in his arms, ever.

CÉLINE: You mean he was more awkward than tender?

THE MOTHER: Exactly. *(Long silence)* He never told me he loved me. Not once. *(She runs her fingers through her hair and sweeps her bangs to the side.)* He'd say I was too good for him. I found that somehow flattering. But I wanted him to show it. He was extremely jealous. I wasn't allowed to wear makeup to work. I wasn't allowed to...to look too elegant. *(Pause)* We never argued about it. I just gave in. At a certain point, what are you going to do? You know it's just going to make things worse. I chose to keep quiet.

CÉLINE: But would you talk about things later? When the dust settled?

THE MOTHER: No, no. There was no talking to him. At all. When we first bought the house, we had a hard time financially, what with his cigarettes and alcohol and everything. And I told him, "Maybe you could cut down a bit." And he answered, "If that's the way it's going to be, I guess we should just move to an apartment." What was I going to do? You do what you have to, to keep the peace. And you end up never saying anything at all. *(Pause)* I trimmed down my grocery budget a little so we could get by. We buckled down. The first years we were married, I still managed pretty nice dinners. After that, you probably found that...that I wasn't exactly a five-star chef. I made things that were quick. You know how it is when you've also got to work, and all the rest.

Scene 12

CÉLINE, THE MOTHER, CHRISTELLE, ÉLODIE, YANN

CÉLINE: Were you two happy in the beginning?

THE MOTHER: The way his dad acted toward us didn't help things, I don't think. When Marcel found out we were getting married, he said to me, point-blank: "You're taking my son away from me."

CÉLINE: He lived with you two, right?

THE MOTHER: He never lived with us. But every Sunday morning, your father would go meet him at the PMU, the horse-racing bar, and then he'd come home drunk around three or four in the afternoon. That was a lot to take. We'd end up arguing every time it happened, because I'd try to say something about it. At a certain point, you stop bothering.

CHRISTELLE: I actually have a lot of memories from around then. There were always people over on the weekends. Mom was telling me on the phone that it was a rough time for her, because it was hard with Grandpa always around. But for me it was pretty great. It was always a party.

CÉLINE: Is that what comes to mind when you think about what Papa was like when you were small?

CHRISTELLE: Parties and games, yeah. That's what all my memories are of. Either people at the house, or our Sunday ritual: going to get Grandpa, then going to a café, and them buying me candy.

THE MOTHER: When you're a kid, you're in your own world. You don't realize what's going on around you.

ÉLODIE: I really liked those weekends with Grandpa. But I wouldn't want that kind of life now, my father-in-law at the house all the time.

THE MOTHER: When Marcel had stomach surgery, he stopped working, so every day when I got home, he'd be at the house—every single day. He'd eat with us, then your father would take him home after supper.

CÉLINE: And he drank every day?

THE MOTHER: Yes, but it was more him being around every evening. I'm not sure you can imagine what that was like. "Is he going to be here this often?" I asked your father a few times. And he said, "He's my dad." "Well, maybe...maybe you could see him a little less?" He told me I saw my dad all the time. But it wasn't the same; my dad was all on his own. My mom had just left him. He needed me. And Marcel wasn't even nice to me.

CÉLINE: What did he say to you?

THE MOTHER: That I didn't know how to raise you girls and that you'd all turn your backs on me one day. He said things about my mom leaving too.

A few years later, talking together in the kitchen, the mother says to her daughter, "Once, your father hit him."

THE MOTHER: We spent a really nice week together, on vacation, the four of us. *(Élodie wasn't born yet.)* Well, other than the fact I had a toothache, but your father went to the pharmacy to get me something for it. I would really have liked that feeling to last a little after we got back. But as soon as we got home that night, he wanted to go straight to see his father at the bistro. I said, "No, Mario. You're staying here with me." He told me he hadn't seen his father in a week, that he wouldn't stay long. In the end he came back late, and Marcel was with him, drunk. He'd spent the whole week at the bistro, waiting for your father. When Marcel saw me, he insulted me. And your father grabbed him by the shirt collar and slapped him. The next day, Marcel was back at the house as if nothing had happened. He never apologized.

Céline doesn't say anything. She thinks over the story for a long time, and the three wounds it hides: the wound of the wife dismayed at being less important than a bar stool; of the grandfather who never lived down the shame he'd inflicted on himself because he didn't dare say out loud how lonely he was; and of the young man her father once was—a young man of twenty-four who couldn't manage, that night or any other, to live up to the love and the needs of others.

THE MOTHER: After that, I couldn't handle him anymore. It didn't matter if he brought me gifts, or some nice bottle of wine… He could afford to give you girls money because he didn't pay rent, since he was living with Jeanne. But that's not what loving someone is. Love isn't measured in the money you give.

Yann comes into the living room, asks the mother if everything is okay and goes back out.

CÉLINE: He seemed worried.

THE MOTHER: He is. He knows I've been having bad dreams for the past few nights.

CÉLINE: Do you want to tell me about the first time you met Yann?

THE MOTHER: We met at a dance when I was nineteen, and the next day he was supposed to meet me and never showed up.

CÉLINE: Ah! So you'd only seen him that one evening?

THE MOTHER: No, a month later, I was at a dance on Bastille Day with my friend Ghislaine. Yann stopped in with his friends. We talked. He really couldn't care less about girls back then. He never explained to me why he'd stood me up. His friend had started going out with Ghislaine, so the two of us went out. We kept seeing each other, but every time he'd say, "You're lucky Alain is going out with Ghislaine. That's the only reason I'm here."

CÉLINE: Were you in love with him?

THE MOTHER: Oh, of course I was.

CÉLINE: But he wasn't in love with you?

THE MOTHER: His friends were the only thing that mattered to him. But after, he thought about it some more. He sent a letter asking to see me again, but I was with your father by then. And I decided to stay with him.

CÉLINE: Papa always felt like he was the runner-up.

THE MOTHER: *(Getting slightly agitated)* I never should have told your father that story. He used to bring it up all the time. But he should have been happy. I chose *him*! Sure I was still a little bit in love with Yann, but I figured no, he's just going to stand me up again and everything. When we saw each other again, we talked about it. Yann was convinced that if I had answered his letter, it would have worked out between us. And he asked me whether it would have changed anything if he'd insisted, if he'd come to my parents' place. I told him, "If you'd come to my parents' place, I would never have let you leave again."

CÉLINE: So, in the end, he should have tried harder?

THE MOTHER: Exactly. After, he told me how he would ride his bike by my parents' house and sometimes he'd see me in the distance. *(Pause)* That was that.

CÉLINE: Maybe it wouldn't have worked out back then, if you'd gotten together.

THE MOTHER: Who knows. That was that, plain and simple. *(She shrugs.)* There are always people you dated when you were young. His was the only first and last name I held on to. And I remembered where he lived. When I was unhappy with your father, I'd think about Yann. That's all. But I never tried to see him again.

CÉLINE: It was your escape.

THE MOTHER: It was my escape. I'd think of the nice times we had together.

CÉLINE: How did you find him again?

THE MOTHER: I looked up his address in the phone book. I told myself, if he hasn't moved, that means he's single. But it took me a while to send him the letter.

CÉLINE: And then he called you?

THE MOTHER: Right away. I sent him a letter on the Tuesday after Easter. I can still see myself mailing it. And he called on Wednesday. I was so excited; Élodie kept saying, "Calm down, Mom." He was very formal at first, he called me Mrs. Meslier, and then by my first name, kept switching back and forth. I'd explained in my letter that I was separated, and he asked, "But have you met someone else?" He was leaving for Brittany that Sunday, but he said to me, "We should see each other before then." I said, "Yes, let's."

CÉLINE: He told you he was married?

THE MOTHER: Yes, he told me. *(Pause)* Wait, no—what did he say? "I have a wife." I felt it already, you know, in the way he said, "We should see each other." I could feel there was something more. And so he told me to meet him Saturday at two, and I never even thought that... I could have wondered if he'd gotten fat, I guess, or something like that. It never even crossed my mind.

CÉLINE: You weren't worried about what he'd think seeing you thirty years later?

THE MOTHER: Not at all. I felt like a teenager. And at two o'clock there he was, waiting in the Atac grocery store parking lot.

CÉLINE: *(With a snort of laughter)* You met in a parking lot?

THE MOTHER: He'd asked whether I knew my way around Plaisir. And I said, "Do you know where Atac is? The grocery store?" He said he did, that he'd meet me in the parking lot.

It had been in this exact parking lot that Céline had met with Philippe a few days earlier, between the cars and the white lines.

CÉLINE: And after that?

THE MOTHER: When we saw each other, we both knew right away. He was having problems with his wife, and it wasn't clear to me if it would last between them. I couldn't be sure. The next day he came to see me, and he asked me to go with him to Brittany. "Since my wife isn't coming because she doesn't get along with my mother, if you want to come, you should. I just need to check with my mother first." And on Monday he called and said, "She said it's all right. You can come." So I went to meet him in Brittany.

CÉLINE: Shit.

THE MOTHER: You didn't know that part, did you?

CÉLINE: No. Or maybe I just forgot?

THE MOTHER: *(Smiling)* I went to meet him in Brittany. We spent three or four days together. The letters I'd written him when I was younger had sat on his bedside table in Brittany for years. His mother finally threw them away when he got married. He told his mother I was the young woman who'd written the letters. So she vaguely knew who I was. And she was well aware how unhappy he was with his wife.

CÉLINE: I was wary of him the first few times I met him, because I knew he was married.

THE MOTHER: Élodie said the same. But he was head over heels in love with me. And completely up front with his wife. He told her straight away. She'd read my letter, so he told her, "This woman's really in love with me. So it's up to you: either you change your ways and stop making life so difficult or I'm leaving with her."

CÉLINE: Do you know what she said?

THE MOTHER: She said, "I'm fifty years old, I'm not going to change now."

CÉLINE: Lucky that was her answer. If she'd decided to change, you wouldn't be together.

THE MOTHER: Maybe he would have stayed. But in the long run...I have no idea. It was still hard for him. His wife did everything she could to make things complicated for us. One night he even called and said, "I can't do this." She was making things too difficult. "Do you care about me?" I asked him. "If you care about me, I'll help you, we'll fight together and you'll make it out okay. But if you don't have feelings for me, that's different. It would hurt, but that'd be that, and we can just drop it."

CÉLINE: Do you think he wouldn't have gotten a divorce if it hadn't been for that phone call?

THE MOTHER: He was thinking about getting one. But he hates hurting anyone. So it was hard for him.

CÉLINE: Separation is hard. It takes years to—

THE MOTHER: But he wasn't alone. When you have someone to help you... When you have to do it on your own, it's much harder.

Later, during the same conversation:

THE MOTHER: When I told my neighbour I was leaving your father, she said, "But have you got someone else?" I didn't.

CÉLINE: And for her that was unimaginable?

THE MOTHER: She didn't get it. She said, "But you know Élodie's going to move out one day." And I said, "Yes, of course she will. But I need to get out of here. I need to save myself."

ÉLODIE: Once Mom and Yann came to pick me up in Maule. They hadn't been together long. I asked them to park at the end of the street so Papa wouldn't see them. But it was bad timing and they drove by right when he was outside. I looked at Papa and said, "We'll talk about it next week." And at the same time, it made me laugh because Papa always said, "Never trust a redhead." So I cracked up when I first saw Yann. Anyways, when I got back to Papa's the week after, I told him, "I'm giving that guy such a hard time." And he replied, "If your mom chose him, I want you to be nice to him." *(She edits the text.)* "If your mom chose him, you accept him." I don't know that he ever managed to show Mom how much he loved her. Because he really did love her.

CÉLINE: I don't know that he ever loved anyone as much as Mom. Sometimes I felt like we came second.

THE MOTHER: I knew he loved me. But sometimes knowing isn't enough. Sometimes you need a person to say it. You need someone to hold you in their arms once in a while. When my father died... I don't know. With Yann, when I'm sad he holds me. But your father wasn't like that. When Pappy died, I just wanted him to hold me.

CÉLINE: And he didn't?

THE MOTHER: No.

CÉLINE: He couldn't stand it if we hugged him either. When his father died, I tried, and he wouldn't let me.

THE MOTHER: You know, when his father died, I was almost happy. I thought, "Now I'll get him back." But that's when he went off the deep end.

THE NEIGHBOUR: At his father's funeral, instead of throwing a flower onto the coffin like everyone else, he threw a cigarette.

Scene 13

CÉLINE, THE MOTHER, PHILIPPE, A NEIGHBOUR,
CHRISTELLE, ÉLODIE, ANOTHER NEIGHBOUR

CÉLINE: At what point do we decide someone is an alcoholic? Is it when the people around them start feeling embarrassed? Are you an alcoholic based only on other people?

THE MOTHER: I think when you start to drink in secret, that's when you're an alcoholic.

CÉLINE: And Papa?

THE MOTHER: He only ever drank in the evening at first. But later, he'd drink all day long. There were bottles everywhere. In the morning, he'd have his cup of coffee, then he'd go into the living room and open the door of the TV cabinet to pour himself a drink.

PHILIPPE: I didn't see him for years. But a few times your mom called me, when your dad had really lost the plot. "You need to get it together," I told him.

A NEIGHBOUR: I never realized he drank. But then one time I saw him park the car and drive right into the pole by the house. He backed up and tried again. Second time, same thing. He didn't hit it that hard, so the fender was fine, but he crashed into the pole three times before he managed to park the car.

CHRISTELLE: I got the feeling the drinking was something that had happened gradually. But Ludovic's death in that accident definitely triggered it in a major way.

CÉLINE: I'm not sure there's a precise moment when Papa started drinking.

CHRISTELLE: It was definitely subtle, and at first it was social. I blame his friends for encouraging him. Though everyone in his family drank too. But I think after Ludovic died…it was more obvious after that. He lost control. It really wasn't normal, all those deaths in the family.

ÉLODIE: There was Grandpa, then his brother Gaëtan died, then Anthony, Noëlle, his boss and Ludovic, all in that same period of time. Ludovic in the airplane was too much for him. He'd shake his fist at the sky and say, "You can't take a child like that, dammit."

CÉLINE: And all those deaths earlier on in his life too. He always used to say he was next on the list.

In this family, tragedies are recounted dispassionately, no differently from small everyday anomalies. The story of a child who boarded a plane that exploded minutes after takeoff. Or, further back, the two cousins Céline and her sisters never met or saw a photo of, they don't even know their names. The older one died in a hunting accident. He wanted to go out hunting with the men. One of the hunters—"he was just a teen," says the mother, a great-uncle in Céline's mind—shouldered his shotgun and pointed it in the child's direction to give him a scare. He forgot he had just loaded the rifle, and he pulled the trigger. A few years later, the other cousin got off a school bus, crossed the street to his mother waiting on the other side and didn't notice a car driving the wrong way down the road.

CHRISTELLE: That's how things were. *(Silence)* He didn't show it; he could seem cold and distant, but deep down he was really sensitive. All those deaths were devastating for him. At a certain point, he just couldn't handle it.

CÉLINE: What couldn't he handle, do you think? Was he afraid of losing the people he loved?

CHRISTELLE: Yeah, I think so. And at a certain point, it was just too much. *(Long pause)* If he'd been able to talk about it, maybe he could have worked through some of it.

CÉLINE: He wasn't from a social class where people talked about things.

CHRISTELLE: I don't know if it's a class thing. Communication doesn't come naturally to most people, and feelings can be just as taboo if you're upper class.

CÉLINE: I don't know that I agree. I always got the feeling it was his social class that killed him—that killed his whole family. The drinking, and how hard life was.

CHRISTELLE: Alcoholics come from all sorts of backgrounds—it's not about class. I can't say what he was thinking, but I think alcohol was an antidepressant for him. It was an escape.

ANOTHER NEIGHBOUR: Drinking is a vicious cycle. It takes everything, starting with your driver's licence, and with that your freedom and independence. Then other people's respect. Your marriage. Your house. Your job. Your health. How can you not be depressed after that?

A NEIGHBOUR: If he'd really wanted to get help, he should have checked himself into a hospital. But he only half-admitted that he had a problem. He used to say he didn't drink any more than the next guy.

CÉLINE: *(Annoyed)* It's true though: everyone was always drinking! None of his friends stepped in. They did the opposite—when he tried to stop drinking so he could get his driver's licence back, his friends would tell him that a drink now and then never hurt anyone.

PHILIPPE: When we saw each other, I'd say, "Nothing for me." That's the truth. I don't touch the stuff anymore. Just coffee. I don't like drinking. He asked me, "Did my wife say something to you?" He thought your mom was behind it, getting everyone to gang up on him. "She didn't say a word. How long have I known you? It shows, that's all." I didn't want him to know it was Élodie who'd talked to me. I was worried he'd take it out on her, the way he did on your mom. He'd gotten kind of paranoid.

Scene 14

CÉLINE, THE MOTHER, ÉLODIE, A NEIGHBOUR

CÉLINE: You wanted to leave by that point?

THE MOTHER: I'd wanted to leave for a long time, but I wanted you girls to be settled first. You left young. And after that I decided to wait until Christelle finished university. And then I waited until Élodie wanted to leave with me. It was hard on her. I waited till she was ready.

CÉLINE: And you'd moved upstairs? Into Christelle's room?

THE MOTHER: Yes, when Christelle left, I took her room. Because I just couldn't do it anymore.

CÉLINE: What couldn't you do?

The mother doesn't answer.

ÉLODIE: At school my stomach would be in knots all day, worrying whether tonight was the night. Papa had gotten more difficult by that point. You could feel the resentment in the house once it was just me and Mom living with him. There were times when I didn't dare come downstairs. I was scared of catching him rooting around in the TV cabinet. When it did happen, he'd always say he was just looking for a video tape.

CÉLINE: You never called him out on it?

ÉLODIE: No, I was scared. *(She starts again, corrects herself.)* I didn't have the courage to.

142

CÉLINE: What were you scared of?

ÉLODIE: He never hit us. If he wanted to hit something, usually it was the wall. But the way he'd look at you…even though it was more sadness than anything, in the end. I didn't want to deal with it. It was hard. *(She adds "sometimes.")* Sometimes it was hard.

CÉLINE: When I was talking to Annette, she kept saying, "I'm sorry, but I can only remember good things about your dad."

ÉLODIE: That makes sense. Because Papa was the type to pull out the charm with everyone else.

THE MOTHER: It stayed in the house. Nobody knew: not friends, not family. Sometimes Élodie would go to the neighbours' when we were fighting with your father. The next day, I'd want to know if they'd asked any questions. But no.

CÉLINE: How long did all that last?

THE MOTHER: A year maybe. Élodie definitely had a rough go of it. I took the brunt of it, but when I couldn't, it was her. He never thought I'd actually leave, so he made life hell. When I left, he didn't stop. I'd given him my phone number, and he kept harassing me. One time I broke down at work: I started shaking, I couldn't calm down. I ended up in the hospital, in the psych ward. I told the psychiatrist who saw me, "I live alone with my daughter, there's no way I can…" He reassured me, "No, it's very clear that you want to get help and get through this." He recommended I see a therapist, and that's when I went to a psychologist, which helped a lot. I would have ended up being committed. *(She snaps a thread dangling from her sweater.)* And he was blackmailing Élodie. He'd call when she was alone at the apartment and tell her he was going to kill himself.

ÉLODIE: He'd say he was going to slit his wrists and put his hands in water—I won't ever forget the details—and that we'd find him dead. I was scared he would go through with it. He'd realized I'd be leaving with Mom. I couldn't stay with him. I'd have been the one to look after the house, and him. It would have been too much.

CÉLINE: It would have been more than too much, it would have been…

ÉLODIE: Unbearable.

THE MOTHER: One year, we spent Christmas at Marc's. I had Élodie and Christelle for Christmas Eve, and they were supposed to go to his house on the twenty-fifth. He called right in the middle of dinner. It ruined the whole night. The girls were in tears. I know it's hard to be alone on Christmas Eve, but… *(Silence. Her expression hardens.)* He tried to get me back. Élodie and Christelle convinced me to go out for dinner with him. But it was uncomfortable.

CÉLINE: There was nothing that would have changed your mind?

THE MOTHER: *(Hesitating)* If he'd changed…

CÉLINE: But that wasn't happening?

THE MOTHER: He stopped drinking after we separated. Cold turkey. He had an episode because of the withdrawal, while he was driving a tractor. He was hospitalized in Mantes. I went to see him twice. The second time, he was outside when I got there. "I leave the hospital every day," he bragged, "get a little air and grab a drink." I couldn't believe it. I told him, if that was the case, then I wouldn't be back again. Are you kidding me? He was leaving the hospital to drink?

ÉLODIE: He told us he'd stopped drinking. We believed him. We figured he had a beer now and then, but that was it. He'd told us that before he got fired from the farm he'd tried to stop completely and he'd started shaking so badly he had to go buy a litre of red wine; the shaking stopped as soon as he drank. And he could get back to work.

THE MOTHER: I was done. The relationship had always been difficult, but we didn't see it while we were together. Near the end... *(Pause)* I could never have gone back. He would have started up again. There was no point.

A NEIGHBOUR: There are people who find their way out though. Some people do find their way out.

ÉLODIE: At the end, he'd changed. I told him what he'd put me through. Not everything, but about the looks he used to give me, we talked about that. He told me, "I must've really put you through hell." *(She replaces this sentence with "It was that bad?")* He didn't remember.

CÉLINE: Do you think, all in all, he had a happy life, in spite of everything?

Élodie crosses out the answer she gave three years before and writes instead: Yes and no. But she still reads her first answer out to the camera.

ÉLODIE: I think there was some happiness. Mom, for one. And us, because he loved us, even if he didn't always know how to show it. I think there was a lot of sadness and pain hidden behind all the drinking. *(She thinks.)* There were happy times, but maybe not enough to make up for the unhappy ones. And I understand him better, as I get older. Life is hard.

Scene 15

CHRISTELLE, A NEIGHBOUR, CÉLINE

CHRISTELLE: I was mad at him for not…for not loving us enough to stick it out. That we weren't enough of a reason for him to fight. But now I've forgiven him for that too. It was his life, after all. *(Silence)* He wanted to die, and that was that.

A NEIGHBOUR: *(To Céline)* He was a rebel, your father.

Plaisir, June 17, 2014

Ms. Céline Huyghebaert
6608 Avenue de Chateaubriand
Montreal, Canada, H2S 2N7

Dear Ms. Huyghebaert,

In response to your request submitted on July 17, 2014,
we regret to inform you that we are unable to provide
the long-form birth and marriage certificates for Mr.
Mario Huyghebaert, as these certificates are not in our
possession.

We suggest that you contact the city hall in possession of
Mr. Mario Huyghebaert's birth and marriage certificates.

Sincerely,

Vital Statistics Officer

And yet all that remains visible and expressible is often the superfluous, the mere appearances, the surface of our experience. The rest stays inside, obscure, so intense that we can't even speak of it. The more intense things are, the more difficult it becomes for them to surface in their entirety. Working with memory in the classical sense doesn't interest me—it's not about stores of memory that we can dip into for facts, as we like. Moreover, the very act of forgetting is necessary—absolutely. If eighty per cent of what happened to us wasn't repressed, then living would be unbearable.

—Marguerite Duras, *Suspended Passion*
(tr. Chris Turner)

OR EVEN DEAD ALREADY

Disappearing

The alarm has sounded: fathers are endangered, or even dead already.
—Lori Saint-Martin

"Don't worry," he said, "it's nothing. Just a checkup."

I answered in a hushed tone because the walls in my apartment were paper thin, and I didn't want my roommate to hear. Hear me talking loudly into the phone to my father, who couldn't hear a thing.

My father.

I don't remember when I first started referring to him that way. There might have been an embarrassing period of time when my friends had all abandoned the word papa and I hadn't managed to do the same, as if I knew it'd be the first of a series of stabs my tongue would deliver to our relationship.

He said, "I can't hear you." And, "Damn phone."

Sometimes I pretend to myself that I replied, "I can't hear you either."

"Damn country," he grumbled.

"Damn country," I repeated. And then I said, "I miss you, Papa."

"What?"

"I love you, Papa."

"What?"

"I love you. I'll call you tomorrow, Papa."

Then I made as though the call was cutting out.

But it probably didn't happen that way. Except for the end. "I'll call you tomorrow." And I didn't.

/

My father. He stands five foot five and a half. He has blue eyes. Grey blue. Tired blue. A beard he trims often but never shaves, except once, on a Saturday. He comes out of the bathroom with smooth cheeks and we cry when we see a face we don't recognize. Us: his girls.

1

His voice said: this body I'm in will be gone before long.
—Ryoko Sekiguchi, *La voix sombre*

The Airport

I'm at the airport when I find out. I remember very little, except my sisters coming toward the gate while everything else—travellers, luggage wheels, cups clinking in the arrivals café, the hands on an improbable clock—is held back like a coughing fit in a movie theatre. A cliché film scene as the sole memory of the first moment in my life as a girl without a father.

On the phone, they never said my father was going to die. But maybe no one ever says that. They said, "No, no, don't worry. They're just keeping him for observation." And then, finally, "You need to get on a plane." They told me I needed to get on a plane, and they wired money via Western Union, like my father had done ever since I'd moved to Montreal. He'd send regular little deposits I viewed as encouragement, but also as the settling of an emotional debt. Reparation for his absence—involuntary and alcohol-induced, but an absence just the same. For that, and the anger that would well up in his eyes, which he imposed on us for so long, as people often do when they're unhappy. Anger I'd so often provoke as a teen, maybe to feel alive, to have a voice, or maybe revenge for the shame I drag around with me, the mark on me. Me, that girl, my father's daughter.

It happens at the airport. Early in the morning. I see my sisters across the terminal and I can tell he's dead by the way they're coming toward me not talking or looking at one another, and by the expression on their faces, and the way their arms reach out slowly, very slowly, for my shoulders. When the scene becomes a memory, the ticking of the clock on the wall superimposes onto it, and masses of movie images fall into the gaps where details have been forgotten. I know without them saying it, but they do anyway: my father—our father—is dead.

And maybe I already know when I'm on the plane, reading a novel where the heroine learns the dying should never be left to die alone in a hospital room. The pills I took to fall asleep drop me into half dreams, where I see my father flying outside the window of the plane; I tell myself my father might already be dead. Of course, at that point it's a fleeting thought, not a body requiring decisions about how it should be buried and with what psalms, even less an absence. I manage to remind myself that I'm going to look after my sick father and it's all a bit crazy. I don't really feel like I can but still I want to do it, to spend two weeks with him in the hospital. I imagine that every evening I pull a cot out from under his bed, stowed like a safety vest under an airplane seat, and I wake up there near him every morning, slipping on clothes and going down to the cafeteria to buy a coffee in a little brown paper cup, walking into the courtyard, sitting on a stone bench, watching patients take drags of their cigarettes or tug at their IVs, going back to the hospital room and bringing with me the smell of wind and tobacco, smiling at my father, who's sitting up now so he can eat his breakfast, cheerfully recounting anecdotes I made up along the way and then sitting down in the visitor's chair, taking a book from my bag, reading aloud very, very slowly, making sure to leave silences for my father to fill.

I wonder where my sisters are in this daydream, whether they'll be spending evenings with us, adding chatter about nothing in particular but reminding us that we are a community. The nurse will come into the room to let us know visiting hours are over. I'll watch my sisters stand up and slip on their coats, give me a pained smile and leave. And I'll stay there in the visitor's chair, with my books, until my father falls asleep, and repeat these motions every day after, even when my father comes home from the hospital and, though I know it won't happen, right up till he dies. I want to read him novels the way people hold the hand of the dying or take them in their arms to show them they're loved, and maybe so something transcendent occurs or, at least, something that eases the suffering. If he has to die I want it to be at peace, and I want to write a story other than the one I'm writing now, to say my father didn't die alone, that his daughters took turns at his side. People would say how lovely, truly, what those girls are doing for their dying father. Out of love.

It's just past 8:00 a.m. on the airplane. Around when my father starts to die. I'd like to remember pressing my face against the window and mouthing words of some sort to him as he flew alongside the plane, so he could read the words he couldn't hear on my lips. Or see me smiling at him. Just that: me smiling at my father, whom I loved. But mostly what I remember is being terrified at the task I'd assigned myself of making sure he didn't die alone.

The List

It would be an exhaustive list, with no commentary whatsoever.
—Marguerite Duras, *Writing*
(tr. Mark Polizzotti)

One day my father gets up at seven in the morning.
One day my father gives me ten francs.
One day my father goes for a drink at the bistro.
One day my father leaves for work.
One day my father answers the phone.
One day my father plays pétanque.
One day my father buys a house.
One day my father drinks his coffee in a bowl.
One day my father lights a cigarette.
One day my father asks what's for dinner.
One day my father mows the lawn.
One day my father fixes the washing machine.
One day my father picks mushrooms.
One day my father is in a bad mood.
One day my father orders an extra slice of bread to go with his
    hamburger.
One day my father takes out his pocket knife.
One day my father shouts to the TV that they should bomb the
    whole lot of them.
One day my father argues with my mother.
One day my father loses his father.
One day my father comes out of the bathroom.
One day my father is generous.
One day my father watches porn.
One day my father is sick of always eating the same thing.

One day my father is young.
One day my father cries.
One day my father is like other fathers.
One day my father catches a bumblebee gathering pollen
    in a bed of lavender between his palms.
One day my father tells the same stories again.
One day my father falls asleep on the couch.
One day my father loses his job.
One day my father smokes weed.
One day my father says you can't earn your daily bread lying on
    your back.

Factory

One day he eats nothing but frozen dinners heated in the microwave for three minutes.

The Telephone

He died in his hospital room at 8:50 a.m., after three days in a coma, at the age of forty-seven. My sisters came to visit on the Sunday with pastries and hope that the worst had passed. In the hallway, they were told he had been in too much pain. The rustling of the paper bag of pastries, obtrusive, like the sound of chips at the cinema. "We've induced a coma." They matched the nurse's stride and followed her into the room. They saw their father lying peacefully in a bed, hooked up to a respirator, and they took a big gulp of air as though it were them breathing through the machine. The nurse suggested they talk to him. "It's not clear how much they can hear, but sometimes they respond." So my sisters sat on the edge of the bed and talked. It felt strange to carry out certain gestures so naturally when they'd never dared before: to take his hand, stroke his arm, quietly tell him they were there for him, they loved him. They told him about their weeks, adding a few jokes to make it seem like none of this was serious. They left the hospital, and Christelle called me. That's when she said, "You need to get on a plane." She mentioned cirrhosis and cancer and hemorrhages and a coma. Not a real coma, she said, it was just to let him rest. I trembled to think how he hadn't been consulted, they hadn't asked before they injected the sedatives whether he'd rather the coma or the pain. I'm sure he would have chosen to stay conscious till the end. My stomach twists as I picture him falling asleep and not knowing it's for the last time. As though it were me pushing the plunger into the syringe.

The doctor called Christelle on Monday morning. Very early. He told her it had been a difficult night and our father hadn't pulled through. She wanted to say something back, but when she opened her mouth, a large stone had gotten lodged between her palate and tongue, so she hung up, took her bag and coat, put on her shoes and went downstairs to hail a taxi. During the hour-long drive to Élodie's, she thought only of the words she would use. *Papa's dead* or *Papa gave up fighting* or *He's gone*. Yes, that's what she'll say—she will hold her little sister tight and tell her, *Papa's gone*. The stone will be able to slide down her throat so death has room to settle, and so that in a few hours, standing in arrivals, she'll be able to say to her other sister, who always wants people to tell it like it is, *Papa's dead*. And she'll say it this way when she tells our mother, who is on a beach in Brittany rekindling the romance of her youth and trying to make up for lost time. And when she tells her, she'll have to recount the whole story again: the tests, the hospitalization, the hemorrhaging, the transfer to another hospital, the coma, death. She'll try to tell it quickly so my mother can't interrupt with questions. *But why didn't you say something sooner?* And she'll let my mother slip into her old role of calling the aunts, uncles, friends, former neighbours. *Mario's passed away*. And many other people will ask the same thing. *Why didn't you...* And she'll say, *It all happened so fast*. Sudden as a car accident—no one saw it coming. Except it wasn't an accident. And our bodies will remember.

I wondered why my sister hadn't told my mother and me sooner, and for a long time I believed it was out of jealousy or resentment, a punishment for our absence—my emigration to Canada and my parents' divorce—two desertions that meant Christelle had to become a substitute mother, sacrificing everything for the ailing patriarch. Only now do I understand that she had no choice, that after weekends sifting through bills, changing sheets, eyeing every corner of the apartment for bottles, encouraging, scolding and worrying, she'd kept on doing it without disrupting anyone's lives, until our father's sickness and his death quickly changed her role from the woman in charge of him to the daughter responsible for her sister's inconsolable sadness at having arrived too late to see her father one last time.

"Most times when people write about their families, it's to get revenge— it's hostile."

It's different for my mother. By leaving her in the dark, my sister spared her the decision of whether to stay in Brittany with her lover or return to her ex-husband's bedside. My mother will never have to feel guilty that she came home too late. What a gift for someone, whose guilt over having survived the marriage already disturbs her sleep and memories.

At the airport, my sisters say, "Papa's dead." Between sisters we don't say *my father* or *our father*. We say *Papa*. He's someone who should be the same for each of us, but isn't. They say, "Papa's dead."

I've never been able to fully take part in effusive airport greetings or goodbyes, but that morning as my sisters tried to enfold me in their arms, their touch like fire, I could have cried out. Not a cry of sadness but of blind rage, excessive and unreasonable—at my father for not waiting for me to get there before he died; at my sisters for not warning me soon enough; at the doctors for having, once again, destroyed a life dear to me; at the time difference because, had it been the other way around, I would have landed the day before; at everyone who abandoned my sick father; at his accursed family and their endless body count; at life, for never cutting him slack; and at myself. Above all, at myself.

The Cry

My father had gone to the hospital of his own accord,
hoping to recover.

—Thierry Hentsch, *Les amandiers*

He had a difficult night.

—The doctor

She barely stifled a cry.

—Marie Depussé, *Est-ce qu'on meurt de ça*

Death is a technical phenomenon obtained by a cessation of care, a
cessation determined in a more or less avowed way by a decision of
the doctor and the hospital team.

—Philippe Ariès, *Western Attitudes toward Death:*
From the Middle Ages to the Present
(tr. Patricia M. Ranum)

And at that moment everything starts to crumble.
Everything starts to crumble.

—Milan Kundera, *Immortality*
(tr. Peter Kussi)

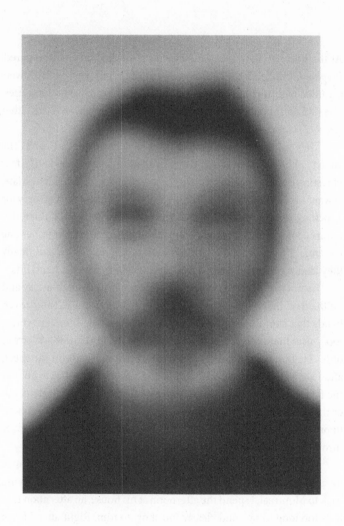

The Sheet

At the hospital, they asked me to wait until the body was prepared. *Prepared.* I imagine the staff in an all-white room where the drawers are filled with small kits labelled Death, Long-Term Stay, Metastases. The kits don't contain medication, just lists of sentences. Your father is gone. He has not been prepared.

They ask me to wait until my father is "ready," but I can't. The anxiety of having arrived too late keeps pulling me forward—the fear of resting my eyes on him too late, placing my hand on his skin too late. "I want to see him." I'm surprised at my firmness. Usually I say sorry for knocking at the door, asking a question, opening my mouth. But today I don't apologize. I'm the daughter who didn't get to see her father one last time; I can demand anything. I ask to see my father, and finally they lead me to a bed draped with a white sheet, which a hand lifts.

It's not me lifting the sheet. People come in and out, that day and on the days that follow. There are hands that carry, unfold and cover, hands that sign things and tap me on the shoulder. There are voices too, voices that explain what to do—because we don't know—where to order the flowers, the notices, the urn, the priest. Hands lift the sheet, and I see his swollen eyelids and his rust-coloured face poking out of the fabric like the innards of a gutted whale. I'm not sure if it's death or the cirrhosis that has lent this colour to his face, or some ointment to preserve the dead, but this is how death imposes itself, a pro boxer throwing punches till the knockout.

Last summer was the last time I saw him. I came back to France for a visit, with a plane ticket he probably helped pay for. Before flying back to Montreal, I spend the afternoon at his house, an afternoon that feels too long to me, and clearly too short to him. Right after I leave his place, he catches up to me in the parking lot in the village, where my mother is waiting for me in her car. He calls out to me, his bright blue eyes brimming with uncertainty. A second later, he tries to appear composed. "That damn country of yours," he says, his voice choked up. My own voice tries to comfort, to say I'll be back before you know it, in a year, and a year goes by fast. But he's more emotional ever since the divorce. Life hits him harder now. Loneliness hits him harder.

We hug, awkwardly. His stiffness betrays how fragile he is, and so I hold back saying more. Then I get into the car with my mother and she drives me back to her place, where I spend one last night before catching my flight. I think of my father, who is probably thinking of me, his daughter who chose to spend her last night somewhere else, and I don't realize this is our last goodbye.

No one can confirm whether this was really the way things went: my father running toward me, his tears. *That damned country of yours!* The clumsy embrace. Him looking at me with his hands in his pockets as the car pulls out of the lot. Nobody can tell me whether heartache has rearranged the choreography of the last moments in a father's series of failed attempts at reaching out to his daughter. No one can assure me that what I remember as *That damned country of yours!* won't later become something like *Stay, I'm not well,* or even, *Stay, I'm going to die.* And still I close the door of my mother's car to leave. Over time, narratives layer over a memory, until the original event is entirely out of reach.

How do we keep these moments intact, before they're muddied by time and other people's stories? Should we record everything, every second of our lives and the lives of others, so we can check our memories against the archives and prevent them from swelling as they're rewritten? I don't have any pictures of my father as a child, let alone of his parents or the rest of his family, but I don't need any. There are so many images circulating already: black-and-white home videos, postcards sent by strangers, paintings and family photo albums—like the two I bought randomly at an auction in Paris. All I have to do is rummage through this collective imagination to reconstruct the landscapes of my father's childhood. What I'm missing are the scenes

I witnessed, the kind never captured on film. The sequence of movements as he stirs sugar into his morning coffee. The series of motions paused in mid-air: an arm reaching out toward me, then dropping. And what I call the final gesture, a close-up of my father's face, lips moving as we hear *That damned country of yours*. The image shakes; it's an amateur film. Then comes the hug, the comforting words, the daughter's tears. She's her father's daughter, crying as she leaves a father with whom she cannot bear to spend more than two hours at a time. But that moment is lost, along with the rest.

It's always so moving, that moment when tears arrive in a work.

—Bertrand Bonello,
on his movie about Cindy Sherman

Touch

In my memory, we went back that afternoon to view the body, but most likely it was a few days later. This time they led us outside, to the large metal door of a single-storey stone building away from the main part of the hospital. At least, those are the details I've registered. I push open the door—it must be heavy—and walk alone down the hall leading to the morgue. It's a big empty room, without windows. My father is lying in the middle, and his body is nothing like the one I had finally been allowed to see when I first arrived.

I step closer. Slowly. I try to cross the space between myself and the dead body—dead, but carefully made up by the embalmer, so skilfully that it's no longer clear whether a death has taken place at all, and you lean down to the height of the bed to be sure the chest isn't rising.

"Do you recognize him?"
"It's my father."

"It's a man with no one inside."

"He's in a better place now."

I slowly reach out and try to breach the gap between my warm hand and his cold body. I haven't touched his skin in so long. That memory layers over the one of my arm reaching out. "Can you put some of this on me?" He passes me a tube of analgesic. He's thrown his back out on the farm. I'm fifteen. He hates asking for help. He's never sick, except the time he mixed up the measurements for the pesticide he was getting ready to spray over the fields: he started shaking with spasms, his vision blurred, he laid down on the parched earth and opened his mouth like a carp gasping for air that won't enter its lungs.

But in the end, he got up and finished the day's work, and didn't go to the doctor. Did he bother to see a doctor back at the forge, when his brother stumbled and planted a reddened slip of metal in his thigh? He tells these stories with something akin to pride. He says he's taken off work just twice in ten, fifteen, twenty years, because of the flu, and then only until the fever broke.

Did he take the day off when we were born?

I want to answer by wringing my hands and shaking them in the air like a woman with too much to do, but the only excuse I can come up with to refuse is my desire to tend to my adolescence, so I keep quiet, take the tube from my father's hands. "You can press harder." My hands obey, pushing into his thin, rubbery skin, like the skin of the frogs my father would catch in the pond in Corrèze, where we used to spend the summer. You needed two sets of hands to kill those frogs: one to hold the frog down against a log while tugging on its feet to unfold the legs, the other to swing the hatchet and cleave through its thighs.

I rub the cream into my father's back, and grit forms under my fingers from the friction, bringing up the particular smell that has soaked into his body from the farm—a smell I once encountered in Montreal as I walked through the aisles of a flea market full of oil-coated tools. The smell of grease and dust, the smell of my father.

Another memory layers over this one. It dates further back. That day, I reach out to touch my father's shoulder as he takes a drink with trembling hands just before we bury his father. I place a hand on his shoulder, shyly, my touch as light as a teen perching on the lap of her date, but a touch nonetheless, and he shoves my hand away and tells me to leave him in peace. It's true, there was the drinking. But it was before, long before, that I first felt an aversion to his body.

I don't remember any of these things as I try to reach out to his dead body now. The memories don't yet exist on the page: the little bits of dead skin rolling across his back and under my fingers, the child he had been and the father he'd tried to be. There's a body stretched out, palms up, mouth slightly open, eyelids one can imagine being closed by a hand accustomed to closing the eyes of the dead. He is clothed. But what is he wearing? Clothes my sisters brought him on their last visit? Or just the white sheet all the way up to his shoulders? Here again, it's hard to recall the specifics of the original scene because of all the images superimposed, all the portrayals of other people's dead laid out for viewings in funeral homes.

I want to take the body in my arms, feel his thin skin one last time, tattoo onto my own skin the smell of his, the smell of grit that will soon be gone for good. I'm certain I could have managed in the hospital, when his face was still the colour of death, if only they'd given me time. But now the makeup has accentuated the harshness of a life spent outdoors. In this display where he is meant to be seen as body not corpse, my father looks almost like he's been brought back to the brink of life. He might fall to one side or the other without warning, and if he fell to the side of life, we couldn't waste the chance to start over, to right all the wrongs and talk things through instead. And that's the only way it could happen because I couldn't let my father die a second time without having changed things, though I'm not sure I could actually change anything. Being afraid of something I should want more than anything in the world—to see my father alive again—throws me into turmoil, equal parts regret and guilt and anguish.

I try a couple times to touch the face, the arm, even just graze them, with the same inhibitions as the teenager rubbing her father's back. Even indirect contact would be enough, through the fabric of the sheet or his shirt, and if I could bring myself to do it maybe some mistakes could be forgiven, some of the wounds could heal. But I can't. Every time I reach out my hand, it stops at the irrational fear that if I touch my father's dead body he'll wake up. The fear that he'll grab my hand, even though I know the only possible thing that could happen is contact with his cold, stiff skin. My hand hovers millimetres away, and panic sets in. My heart is about to leap out of my chest.

I give up, step back. I lean against the wall, in this empty room apart from the hospital, where bodies come through one after the other before they are placed in coffins. And I draw. In pencil. The man lying there, facing a ceiling of stone, cement or wood—I no longer remember which. I draw a mouth half open and a long grey thought escaping it.

Our archives should be more than happy moments. The sad moments, hard ones, the failures and deaths, are as much a part of us as the weddings, birthdays and vacations. Some might say that pain paralyzes, that these events are too devasting for anyone to want to take out a camera. But if we can step away from the feeling of joy for a moment to record it, couldn't we do the same for sadness? Couldn't we pause it for the time it takes to snap a photo? I find myself wishing I had a more detailed record to help me remember my father's corpse, more than just the mental images and pencil sketches. Is that so unseemly? Should I run from the body and the image it forms in my memory? Is there too great a risk that it will replace all the birthdays in our family photos?

> "Running away is never the only answer, of course. Yes, it's good to face things. But how deep do you go? Do you pick up a scalpel, slice open the body, examine the entrails, do scans and pore over them, run tests and pore over them, then dissect and divide and decorticate?"

> "[If] you want to get to the very depths of the dissected human body, you must move either the body or your eye to examine it from all directions. From above, below, and from the sides."

> "For a long time we see only one side of a person's personality, because for reasons of self-preservation we do not wish to see any other, I thought, then suddenly we see all sides of their personality and are disgusted by them."

Or maybe not disgusted, but disappointed. Because none of all this allows us to uncover a person's true nature.

In the morgue, visits are elliptic. The visitors glance at the bed and tell me they'd rather remember him alive. I wonder about the risks of letting death settle like this, in its own time, and whether I might forget the living man. But for me, staying by his side accomplishes the opposite. It's a way to record something tangible before the rest disappears, one last impression of my father's existence, like in ancient times when we would cast moulds right from the faces of our dead.

And the smell of those who've left? Who preserves it?
                    —Ryoko Sekiguchi, *La voix sombre*

1

The photo is dated 1997. The more I look at it, the more I realize it's impossible to bring this man fully into focus.

The Ceremony

Then there was the ceremony. Different from the funeral scenes from American movies that still lingered in my mind. There was no friend, sister, daughter or ex-wife saying something awkward, no speeches read into the mic looking out over the nave. Just two or three high-pitched, quavering voices cantillating church songs and the prayers orchestrated by the priest—pious words: *He was one of God's children; He joins his mother, father, his brothers Patrice and Gaëtan...; He has reached the end of his journey on this Earth and You shall welcome him into Your house; Father, have mercy on him; You are with God now.* Words that told us now he was better off, when in truth he was no better or worse off, just indefinitely absent.

I'd wanted to read the Book of Job, which seemed the religious text closest to the bare and unvarnished truth of what my father's life had looked like near the end—a small, sick man bent by pain that had struck without reason. I wanted to read the Book of Job from start to end, my mouth full of venom that would pour into the pews as the congregation sat there stunned; these were not the sugared words they'd come to hear. The priest refused, offering a potpourri of New Testament scraps to pick from instead. So I backed out. In a few short days, I'd gone from the daughter who'd been unable to see her father one last time to the daughter who'd lived far away while he was sick—an even lesser status and one that, above all, meant my choices could be called into question. It's a comfort to think one day I'll be old enough to make my own decisions and impose them on others. I'll choose the place, the priest, the song and the reading. But the truth is, it never comes, that moment when we stop fearing the authority of institutions and traditions. Ceremonies will continue to impose their flowers and songs, the appropriate clothes. The exact, composed gestures. We'll place ourselves where we must. We'll act in the ways permitted. Only later, when we're alone, will we allow ourselves to fall apart.

The funeral went smoothly and as planned, in memory of a man who'd ceased to exist much longer ago than anyone dared to admit. There was a coffin and a priest, a crowd gathered in a church square. Everyone talked about where they'd been when they'd heard "the news," how shocked they were, though they'd been expecting it for some time. "Maybe it was suicide," they said. No one mentioned the role we'd all played, each of us, with our small cowardly acts, and even our encouragements, insisting on pouring him a glass of wine because, go on, it doesn't count, and it's too important an occasion to forgo the bottle we all need so badly, but none of us as much as he needs it.

We made it seem as though the way things ended didn't concern us. We were losing a loved one, and that was sad. We promised to keep his memory alive, to speak of him often, though what we would speak of we wouldn't say, surely things we needed to remember: stories that pumped a pleasant syrup through our veins in place of the cheap wine he used to drink to forget himself. We would construct the image of someone who had lived life to the fullest, and it would be missing so many pieces—a mosaic of a man we'd all stopped seeing because he was hard to be around or his sadness was so grating we could no longer stand his company. We would construct a person from the memories of before: the joking around, the petty thefts in his twenties that earned the admiration of his friends, his sense of humour. We would patch up any holes in the stories with his legendary generosity. All this out of respect for the dead, and maybe also to buy into a self-help brand of positive thinking, because bitterness and reliving the past, anger, defeatism and pessimism are all risks to our acid–base balance—they can produce free radicals. Or they are, at least, impediments to a long, happy life.

At the end of the service, each daughter was supposed to get up, walk to the coffin, stand beside it to face the congregation and place a daisy on the lid. Élodie stood up. She approached the coffin, put her flower down and cried all the way to the exit. It was my turn next, but I couldn't pull myself to my feet. Something in me resisted, the thought of my father still there with us holding me there. Or maybe I knew my father would have balked too, in the same situation, and would have chosen some jarring, personal act instead, surely something irreverent. I tried to keep still and quiet, to not give in. But in the end, I got up. I tossed the flower onto the coffin without looking at the pews, then ran outside and away from my shame. Overcome by sadness, they must have thought.

"A woman I didn't know came over to me and said, 'He's happier where he is now.' I stared at this woman until she moved away. I still remember the little knob of a hat she was wearing."

After the ceremony, the crowd began to thin. It was late and we all had work to do, errands to run, dinner to make, fatigue piled up. We drove through the countryside, a tiny procession of two cars on its way to incinerate a body. It was a weekday. We had traded stories in the church square. Already, that was a lot.

Dr. SAIDEH KHADIR, M.D.
Lic. 98-026-3
CLINIQUE MEDICALE D'URGENCE
1814 EST, BOUL. ST. JOSEPH
MONTREAL, QUE., H2H 1C7

TEL. 523-3563

Pour........ *Krzygorkart.* C.

Adresse..

℞   Date........ 10-4-12

lurme artificielle

| REPETATUR | 1 | 2 | 3 | 4 | 5 | | NR |

Prescription for artificial tears.

The Ashes

When you walk into the crematorium, there's a guest book, like you might find in an art gallery or on a table in a hotel lobby. You might half expect to read *thank you, what a nice exhibit, what a comfortable room*. But instead there are only I-love-yous, each written for someone different, scribbled here because there was no time to say them, and suddenly the words felt too heavy to hold.

On the small television screen on the waiting-room wall, we saw my father's body entering the oven. What a relief, my mother said. At her niece's cremation, they had been there in the room behind a single pane of glass. Amid the talk of oven doors opening and flames swallowing coffins, I couldn't help but think of what was done to the Jews, the attempt to deny their existence to the point of disappearing its ultimate proof: the body.

In the waiting room, they played the music we'd chosen. I thought about how bodies are always burned to music, maybe to drown out the crackling of flesh and bone. Only seven of us were present: my mother, Christiane; my sisters, Christelle and Élodie; my aunt Annette; my cousins Grégory and Alexandre; and me. We barely spoke.

They gave us the urn.

I'd had a long time to look at the body, to observe every inch of the yellowed skin of a face bloated by cirrhosis, hoping I would remember each detail. But I couldn't bring myself to touch the urn they gave us, just like I couldn't touch my father's skin in the morgue. Holding the urn meant still holding him, and I was afraid. Afraid of feeling something, afraid the ashes were still warm.

Did the urn have a plaque? A copper plaque engraved with *here lies* and his name and dates of birth and death? Or did we decide it was a waste of money? I'm not sure. And I'm not sure whether we made the right decisions, if it's what my father would have wanted. Would my father, who'd never set foot in a church, have wanted the ceremony we'd organized? Were we like all those couples who choose to marry before a priest, so that the moment is more than a mere detail in their life story? If we could have asked him, I don't think he would have wanted it—any of it. To die. To die and be placed in a box. Die and be replaced by writing and photos and nothingness.

A few months later, my sisters brought the urn to Montreal, so we could empty it into the Saint Lawrence River. I touched the ashes in the end. The ashes had been dead for a long time. That's what comes to mind. The ashes were finally dead.

The Apartment

I hadn't touched the body, but I would have needed to touch every object he owned. To breathe in the smell of farm and grit. Sleep in his bed with the dead skin cells. Eat the leftovers in the fridge. But we had other things to deal with: the paperwork, the formalities, the estate, the apartment. At my mother's house, a pile of papers sat waiting on the living room table. I kept glancing at them every time I came into the room.

> *Last known address:*
> *Date and place of birth:*
> *Date and place of death:*
> *Father's name:*
> *Mother's maiden name:*
> *Bank account number:*
> *Branch address:*
> *Social security number:*
> *Last employer:*
> *Previous year's income tax statement:*

The empty spaces seemed to have been left for me—I didn't know the answers—accusing me of being absent those last years. So I left the forms there on the table.

The apartment had to be cleared out. All of it. His drawers, cupboards, bed, his trash cans, his mailbox, his fridge. Boxes packed to give away. The beer-glass collection for Philippe. A set of dishes for cousins who had just moved into their first apartment; I imagined them living with these pieces of my father. The two of them having dinner, his plates on the table. His forks. His spoons. His loneliness. His bitterness.

There was a big blue dumpster outside the living room window, from which all his other possessions were thrown, with a loud *bong* when they landed. The others threw things. Not me. I didn't throw anything out the window. I didn't pack the boxes either. Whenever I went near a box, it was to unwrap the objects inside it, as though it were Christmas. I scanned the room, trying to memorize a life before it disappeared into the dumpster. The life of this man I didn't know. ("But you do know him!" my mother objected.)

I lifted a pair of pants that had been left to soak in a basin, and my sister let out a little cry. The jeans were covered in blood. "It's okay," I said. I wanted to feel like it was no big deal for someone to touch their father's blood. I imagined his body stretched out in the morgue, the gaping mouth of death and the skin of the still-living—skin that seemed to be alive yet static and that I couldn't bring myself to touch—and the small, ordinary objects around me become precious. They painted a portrait of my father much more faithful than the one time would produce. But there were too many people in the apartment and too much commotion for me to pause, take out my camera and capture the way the furniture was placed, or an image of dirty dishes in the sink, the clumps of dust or the mattress laid out on the bedroom floor.

"I had this idea of saving the things from the past that can't be saved. How do you save something that exists only in your mind?"

I wandered around the apartment. All these people with their sleeves rolled up. *Bong. Bong.* His belongings falling into the dumpster. My need to take my time. Regrets at not having had a single moment alone in the apartment to take in the surroundings. My obsession with touching the objects around me. A desire to keep everything for myself. I would have liked to make a big pile in the middle of the room, a big pile of insignificant objects, and lie down next to them and forget the noise around me.

"But where are we supposed to put it all when you go back to Montreal?" We could have put "it" in boxes that could have been stored somewhere. My sisters had shelves in their closets, basements in their homes. Yes, but they didn't want to leave with all of it—the weight of my father. That's where the friction began, in our different ways of carrying grief. Christelle, who'd been crushed under obligation, wanted to get rid of it, every bit of the past, to throw it out right away. And to live right away. And I could barely breathe with the guilt of not having been there, not having known how to love him as he was—and she hadn't known how to either, she hadn't loved him drunk and short-tempered, but she had stayed with him anyway. And she couldn't believe I would ask her to keep looking after my father, what was left of him, to clear space among her own things to make room for my father's old knick-knacks, while I flew home to live my life in Montreal.

I wasn't cleaning. I was watching everyone else, my eyes burning with questions and livid, livid, livid that no one dared look me in the eye, only at the floor. I opened my mouth to say something. This time I opened my mouth instead of leaving with a shrug, as though it didn't matter to me, like I usually did, and regretting it later. I opened my mouth so the father who had died would be my father too, the sadness would be mine too. The words exploded out of my mouth. My sister yelled at me to be quiet. Accused me of having left. We trotted out old resentments.

I can't recount the argument. We are no longer those same people. And I don't think about the people we were anymore. I've forgotten them.

I slammed the door behind me and nothing else happened except that I went to smoke on a stone bench in a village in Île-de-France, while my sisters finished dealing with the apartment, with their father, with their dead father's belongings still falling from the window. *Bong*. A friend of a friend came out to ask me to suck it up, to make it easier on my sisters. I looked at him, stunned. I wanted to slap him. But I just sat there. It was as though I'd lost something important, something tangible, because I'd moved away. Lost my right to a place here. So I left. I vanished amid all the objects flying out of my father's window.

Inventory of Objects from His Apartment

A mattress, a bedside table, an emerald ring, three pipes, a driver's licence, a piece of ID, a passport, a credit card, a chequebook, a black leather wallet, a box of matches, identical pairs of jeans with and without holes, a parka, a tie, a yellow shirt, branded T-shirts, a beige wool vest, two navy-blue sweaters, a light-blue sweater, cut-off jean shorts, a wedding suit, various sweatshirts, underwear, a bathrobe, a scarf, a belt, a watch, rope, a boiled-wool blanket, a duvet, two pillows, two top sheets, two fitted sheets, two duvet covers, a pair of curtains, a collection of beer glasses, a Laguiole knife, a mushroom knife, Johnny Hallyday and Bob Marley records, all the Gaston Lagaffe and Asterix and Obelix comics, a few issues of *Picsou* magazine, a book about mushrooms, lighters, a road map, a television set, a VCR, several films on video cassette, a microwave, a fridge and a freezer, a hot plate, a coffee maker, a washing machine, a set of cutlery and plates and glasses, salad bowls, several pots and pans, a colander, a faience bowl with his name on it, a can opener, a corkscrew, a pepper mill, a cutlery tray, a toaster, Tupperware containers, a few tea towels, a litre of sunflower oil, pasta, rice, a melon, a few cans of food, an opened pound of butter, a stale half of a baguette, bottles of red wine, a bottle of port, a napkin ring, a watering can, a mirror, a jar full of lapel pins, two armchairs, four kitchen chairs, a Formica table, a TV cabinet, three hand towels, a toothbrush, a bar of soap, some wire, nail clippers, a comb, beard scissors, a first-aid kit, some medication, a tube of toothpaste, dry-scalp shampoo, several pairs of worn shoes, a pair of slippers, a set of keys, a photograph of him as a child, a photo album, four stamp albums, a collection of silver coins, a stereo system, a type case, a telephone, a bellows, a poker, wood planks, a circular saw, hammers, a level, cutting and non-cutting pliers, two electric drills, nails, bolts, screws and screwdrivers of various sizes, a chainsaw, two fishing rods, a spool of fishing line, hooks and lures of all kinds, spoons, flies and other bait stored in a tackle kit with two trays, a wooden cabinet with glass doors, a roll of Scotch tape, a bedside lamp, a clock radio, a pack of white envelopes, a rabbit tail key chain, some loose change, an umbrella, two TV remotes, a dog collar, some cards on the fridge door, an air rifle.

I'm also an object.
—Clarice Lispector, *A Breath of Life*
(tr. Johnny Lorenz)

Second-hand

When his brother died, my father inherited his collections—the silver coins, the stamps, the beer glasses. He kept them like he played the lottery: with the despair of a poor man who knows his only way out is a stroke of luck. The stamps were the most prized of all. There were stamps from China, Australia, even Canada. I was allowed to play with them when I was little (I pretended to be interested in stamp collecting and subscribed to a specialty magazine, but I spent most of my time taking the stamps out of their albums and sorting them into separate envelopes, trying to reorganize them into heterotopic arrangements that always got the better of my logic; whether I sorted them by theme, colour, country or size, I'd always end up with one stamp left over—a stamp that could fit into multiple categories—and I would have to rethink my whole system). My father kept telling me that one day those stamps would be worth a fortune. I don't dare imagine what he'd have thought to see me shove the albums into a bag one morning and go to Paris to have them appraised. Back then, I thought everything had to be spent, and at once, since it was only today that existed.

My father's mania for accumulation bordered on hoarding. He brought home everything he found, and kept it. Every scrap of electrical wire, every screw, every nut and bolt was collected and sorted into drawers by size, shape and colour. The day for large furniture disposal was marked on his kitchen calendar. In villages in France, furniture and other large objects can only be thrown out on certain dates; on those evenings, my father waited till nightfall so he could scour the streets for discarded treasure. He'd proudly tell us how he'd snatched such-and-such a piece right from under the nose of an antique dealer who was pretending to forage in the garbage next to him, hoping my father wouldn't know the value of what he was holding. No such luck; my father overvalued every trinket. Over time and after the addition on the house, he soon had an entire room for the items he'd amassed. Before that, the objects used to leave with him on Monday morning to be stored in the canteen at the farm. Sometimes they returned months later, stripped down and restored, to our living room or a friend's.

Maybe hoarding is the expression of a transference neurosis heightened with every new loss. The belief is that by accumulating objects, memories and friends, one day all of it will create a place to shelter, where there's nothing to be afraid of anymore—not death or the emptiness that has been there since childhood. My father was trying to hold on to something that slips away fast. I was too little to understand. I was participating in the squandering of things. I never, ever told him his stamps were worthless. That all it had taken was a quick glance from an expert to know.

Do other families have deaths accumulate in such high numbers that they say *See you next time* at funerals, since wakes are more frequent than celebrations? They're all dead, all the people my father was close to: his parents, his brothers and sister, half of his nephews. As though they carried an invisible mark. A mark that disappeared with him when he died, I tell myself.

The last time I visited my aunt Annette, she gave me her photo albums. I examined the oldest pages, especially the ones with photos of my parents. There's a barbecue, makeshift tables, a child in a pedal car, my parents holding hands, my mother smiling, the point where her shoulder touches the shoulder of her friend, the two of them standing close like teenagers, my aunt bringing her hands to her temples and laughing. But no sign of a mark. I leaf through the pages and they're so so happy, so happy and so young that I can't help thinking that there's no curse at all behind all the drama and deaths, that maybe there's no mark, only weariness, weariness and disappointment, weariness and age, and it broke their trust in the future and used it up. It's like how we sometimes scratch out the faces of people in photos who we don't want to remember anymore. And time, which brings none of what was promised. Time, which has fatigued the faces in these old pictures and erased their youth, is descending on the photos of my own youth. At this very moment, some of my friends are likely falling victim to this dark magic.

Family albums are maybe less a story of happy times and more about how we self-sabotage, how the horizon narrows and choices become scarce until it feels like there aren't any left at all.

June 1975: The engagement.

Madness

In the beginning, grieving physically hurts. For weeks after I get back to Montreal, I struggle against a pain so immense it engulfs the space around me. It's almost July first, moving day in Quebec. I wait out the passing days in an empty apartment I'll soon have to leave. My roommate moved out already, with the furniture and the appliances, while I was incinerating my father—we can say *while I was burying my father* but it's not acceptable to say *burning my father* or *reducing my father to ashes*. I've moved my mattress to the narrow living room, so the glow of the street lights can keep watch through the night and chase away the ghosts. I sit cross-legged on my bed and eat things I don't need to cook. I don't sleep. At all. I stare at the ceiling, listening to crackling voices over the clock radio.

In my bedroom, a convalescing pigeon dirties a carboard box with greenish shit. I found the pigeon on the corner of Laurier and Saint-Laurent. It was desperately trying to climb onto the picnic table where I was sitting. I couldn't help but see it as a sign, my father looking out at me through its wounded pigeon eyes. So I made a nest for it out of my sweater and walked it over to my ex's apartment nearby. On the way, I pictured the scene at the door, when we see each other again: I'll be someone different, and he'll be someone who still loves me. He'll open the door, and when he sees me he'll say, "There you are." Just like that.

"Quick, we have to do something for my pigeon."

"But I...you..."

"Do you have a box? Cardboard? Some straw? Sunflower seeds? Grass? How are you doing?"

He'll disappear into the apartment, and I'll be grateful he doesn't ask how I am too. He'll come back with a carboard box three times as big as my pigeon. I'll poke holes in the lid. He'll pick up my pigeon, place it in the box. He'll suggest that we put my sweater on the bottom so the pigeon can smell my scent and feel safe, while he goes out to buy some straw and seed. It'll feel as though we saw each other just the night before, my father's death wedged between two days. We'll walk to the pet store, and from the pet store back to his apartment, seed and straw in hand, and then we'll put it in the box.

"Look, he's closing his eyes," he'll say.

"Do you think he's about to die?"

"No, no. He's just falling asleep."

"It smells good in here."

There will be the smell of something cooking, and he'll ask if I want to stay for supper. And maybe I'll even say yes. Maybe I'll sit down on the couch, and he'll bring me a big steaming bowl that I'll pick at, not really hungry. And maybe I'll ask to stay the night, looking at the floor, just one night, I swear, and nothing will happen, me and the pigeon will be gone first thing, before you've even opened your eyes, I promise. And he won't answer but he'll sit down next to me and stroke my hair, maybe my neck too, and maybe even my shoulders and my breasts. My ex looks like my father. When he can't sleep, he drinks like Papa used to. He says that drinking Calvados is like biting into a big green apple. No worse.

It didn't happen that way, of course. My ex was at his new girl-friend's house. It was his roommate who opened the door. His room-mate seemed happy to see me, and even happier to help, as though he knew deep down the story was much sadder than it seemed. He found me a box and asked if I wanted to stay to eat, but I said no. I was on the verge of tears, I didn't want to tell him my father was dead because it would feel like I'd sullied the whole story by reducing it, just like that, to a single sentence. I went home, fed my pigeon some sunflower seeds, gave it some water and sprinkled fresh grass in the bottom of the box.

This will be the first move I can't manage in a taxi, since I have too many things. I have a couch, a dresser, a shelf, a coat rack, a bookshelf, a compact washing machine, a suitcase of books, a mattress and two bags of clothes. It's not much, when you think about it. And I think about it often, while staring at the living room ceiling. *Bong. Bong. Bong.* I think about the sound of things flying through windows and I stare at the ceiling all night. I listen to the radio and smoke one cigarette after another. I look up at the ceiling and beg my father to come back. It seems crazy, but some part of me believes he will. He has to. He has to speak to me. One last time. I'm not equipped for perpetual sadness. Breakups have been my only heartbreak—heartbreak that can lift momentarily with one more chance or one last explanation. So I sob. I sob and beg who knows what divine authority stuck inside my ceiling to turn back time. I eat on the floor. I let out little cries. I'm an animal. I don't sleep anymore. I smoke. I don't think I'll ever sleep again. I can't even manage to go outside to walk around like a madwoman, these thoughts in my head.

During the day, traces of his death are visible on my face, but people are understanding because I can still function. My secret life as a madwoman in my mind. Life goes on unchanged. It's the same, exactly the same, as before—the same size bus tickets, the same shop-window displays as last month, the same coffee-shop conversations—and no one is surprised. Others talk and I participate from afar. I learn how to better hold things inside. Things and thoughts that have become obsessions since my father died. Often, I think about his final moments before death. How can I know for sure that he drifted off slowly and unaware? That at the last minute, he didn't panic?

In a strange turn of events, in the month before my father's death, I'd been obsessed with a Tolstoy novella that tells the tale of an ordinary but awful tragedy. Ivan Ilyich is a bourgeois man torn away from life's simple pleasures by an illness that draws him closer to death each day. To understand the origin of the story, I began reading Tolstoy's letters, and in delving into them I discovered that he was someone familiar with death, just like my father. When he was two years old, his mother died, and when he was eight, his father. Then, over the years, his grandmother, his two aunts, his brothers Dmitri and Nikolai and four of his children. After spending a month at Nikolai's bedside, he wrote in a letter to a poet friend: "A few minutes before he died, he dozed off, then suddenly came to and whispered with horror: 'What does it all mean?' He had seen it—this absorption of the self in nothingness."

The story of a dying man who panics on seeing death has now layered onto my father's story. I imagine him in his hospital bed. After lunch, the nurse checks on him. She gives the drip two little flicks to get the line flowing again, takes his temperature and blood pressure, replaces the bag of fluids and fills in the chart. But no one checks on him after that. The drip blocks.

That's when my father wakes up. He opens his eyes, looks around, recognizes the room—a hospital room—and tries to speak. In his confusion he doesn't call the nurse or doctor, he calls for his wife, the woman he spent so long loving so poorly. Because of the coma he doesn't remember they're no longer together. She still remembers, but she would like to forget the rest, all those years of a marriage that didn't deliver on the promise, and act as if there had only ever been Yann.

Papa would sometimes bring him up, the man who'd left my mother, and how she, jilted and afraid of ending up alone at the age of twenty, settled for my father, who loved only her. We chalked the story up to his paranoia, a paranoia that grew as the years passed, until conspiracies overwhelmed his daily life and he started keeping an air rifle in the entryway, between the door and the shoe rack, just in case.

Once, at a local dance, he and his friends cornered a guy who'd dared to slow-dance with my mother. When they shoved him, the guy thought it was a joke at first. Doubled over, his hand crushed under a heavy leather shoe, he smiled stupidly up at my father, who smiled back.

After she divorced, my mother found the courage to see if her dreams were still viable. She got back in touch with her first love. She's racing to cram as many happy hours as she can into a love story that she hopes, one day, will be full enough to erase twenty years of marriage. And we, her daughters, hope so too. Not so she will forget, but for the past to stop chasing her, so she can finally be happy.

For the time being, of this escape for survival that my mother is in, my father knows nothing. He knows he's alone. The pain that brought him to this hospital room hasn't left. The smell of putrefaction saturates the room. His two daughters in France have told him everything will be okay. It's just a few tests. But he's lost count of the days. And there's a smell. It's him, his body. His body in the process of dying. He's dying. And no one is with him. He knows this too. He tries to remember a time when he was happy. He's sure such a time existed. But the pain, the medication and the humiliation feel much closer.

He has to search back in his memory, further than the memory of evenings sitting in the armchair in his little apartment in Feucherolles, where nothing—except maybe a picture or card stuck to the door?—can keep him from forgetting he once had friends and a family. He has to go further back than the postcard his daughter sent him that year. Further back than being humiliated on the construction sites where he'd gotten odd jobs after being fired from the farm he'd worked at since the age of nineteen. Further back than the day he waited for hours at his sister's doorstep while she pretended not to hear him knocking. Further back than the camp cot he unfolded in a guest room in Garancières so he wouldn't have to sleep alone in the bed where he'd once slept with his wife—and this pain in his belly! Further back than the deed of sale for the house, further back than the image of his friends coming through the door not daring to say hello, taking out the furniture one piece at a time, and the boxes his wife points to. Further back than the rage that won't subside ever since he lost his licence. Further back than the sermon the judge delivered at his hearing, and further than his response, *I drink no more than anyone else*. Further back than the dent in the living room door from his fist, after too many arguments with his wife and girls. Further back than the day his daughter threatened to jump from the second-floor window if he didn't let her leave.

Where is it, and when? Where is this image of happiness? Perhaps in the springtime scene of a Sunday picnic behind the building site of their future house? They spread out blankets in the tall grass in the yard, grass so high the girls wander through it like a labyrinth, shouting and laughing wildly. On the blankets, they have laid out tomatoes, hard-boiled eggs with mayonnaise, bread, ham, cheese and wine. He looks at the garden and thinks how he has everything he's always dreamed of. It's not a painful thought then, because, at twenty-eight, he's convinced that life only gets better, only gives more. He started out with almost nothing: a mother taken by tuberculosis, an alcoholic dad, the bitterness of winters in an unheated home, so cold that his brothers and sister and he preferred to get dressed outdoors. His older brother has died, and three of his nephews too, before he even meets Christiane, this wonderful woman who's afraid she isn't loved—and God, does he love her—with whom, ever since, he's accumulated birthdays, children and now this house.

Yes, that's where the image of happiness dates back to: the girls wading through the tall grass in the yard, he and his dad talking about the deck they'll build next summer, his wife napping in the shade of a slender birch. He remembers how he had never been so happy, and then the relentless decline that led to the hospital bed where he will die, and he wishes someone would hold him. That someone would hold him as he held his dog Polka while she died a slow death by poison. He'd found her in the farmyard huddled in a ball and rushed her to the vet. In the car, she lay on his lap as he drove, whining and swinging her head between convulsions, as though searching for an explanation. My father realized it was too late. He pulled over to the shoulder of the road. He looked straight into the dog's eyes, stroked her fur. That's how Polka died, reassured, eyes and body wrapped up in his.

I don't ever stop thinking of all this, as other people talk in the street, as my pigeon lines its cage with droppings, as life continues to stay the same. Every day I change the soiled cardboard box, I put in more grass, fresh water and seeds, and I think about my father. The box is open. The pigeon doesn't leave. Not even to walk around the room. I watch it for hours. I watch it watching me. It closes its eyes. It opens its eyes. It drinks. It eats.

Sometimes it lets me stroke the top of its head. I think of my father lying alone in his hospital room, looking at a life that imminent death has him reviewing with eyes wide open, eager to find meaning. That, and the cry he lets out.

Maybe it's a cry of terror. The kind of cry we let out when death is so certain that the body, refusing to give in, has no other weapon. Sometimes I tell myself it's a cry that serves only to stun the person uttering it, to cover the assailing chaos of memories when no one is there to distract them. The buzz of phony excuses—*I was drowning in work, It wasn't a good time*—and vague promises—*See you soon?*—of those who desert you but won't admit it. The sound of the phone ringing, the taking to task, *Someone*—who exactly?—*saw you staggering home.* And disappointment—*I thought you quit drinking*—when all my father wanted was to be a guy who grabbed a beer with his buddies in the village on weekends, a funny, likeable guy who loved life. He yells; the cry distorts his face. Fear is not a quiet feeling.

Finished

And I often wonder, my dear, what he thought about when he realized that he was about to die. Some regret? A face he had once caressed? Or already the abyss?

—Lydie Salvayre, *The Company of Ghosts*
(tr. Christopher Woodall)

In order to understand what happened to my father, I must imagine waking in a fever and making out the letters that spell imminent death.

—Siri Hustvedt, *Yonder*

"It's finished!" someone said over him.

He heard those words and repeated them in his soul. "Death is finished," he said to himself. "It is no more."

—Leo Tolstoy, *The Death of Ivan Ilyich*
(tr. R. Pevear and L. Volokhonsky)

So He Wouldn't Have to See Me

Or maybe he opened his eyes and saw the time on the clock on the wall in front of him. It was eight o'clock. The thought was hazy, but he remembered the voices of his daughters telling him Céline would arrive Monday. So my father died on purpose that morning, so he wouldn't have to see me.

"That's ridiculous. That's not what happened," Christelle would say, during a recorded conversation.

The Trip to Scatter the Ashes

They didn't tell anyone what was inside the box in the trunk. They'd all driven up from Montreal, death packed in the back alongside the luggage.

Céline hoped the trip would release more than ashes, open something stuck inside her, and maybe in all of them, since she'd heard the words "Papa is dead." Her father, theirs, dead the same day. They had turned on the radio to try to make things pleasant. Or maybe she dreamed that the music, a Bonga song from their album *Angola*, would pop the bubbles of silence crushing their chests, bubbles so big they filled the whole car, and would soon buckle the roof and break the windows.

One of them would need to tell a story. *Do you remember that time...?* A story that would make them laugh and lead to another story and another after that, and maybe out of this sequence of stories some more painful memory would surface. At first, they'd be afraid of it. They'd want to take a step back. But they'd keep going and find a strange pleasure in talking about what hurts. Each of their versions would somehow slide into the gaps in each other's memories. They'd realize they were trying to write a history for all three memories combined, a shared history. They could finally discard the details, since it's the details that hurt, the remorse that returns each night in a new form, shame that settles into the street lights—all the details that are too much and cannot be shared. And then, maybe the night after, other memories would come, memories that don't shift based on other versions but that shatter on impact: *That day you shouldn't have... He thought that you...* And then there would be tears, and their anger would empty as they cried and ready them for the moment when they would have to let their father go, all three of them now hiking a trail in Pointe-de-l'Islet, in Tadoussac. As for what was next, they wouldn't know what it would look like. In the movies, we never find out what happens after.

But for now, the car held them tight against their fears. Céline was quiet. She didn't speak, despite the sentences she thought she might say to stir up bad memories, didn't even jot them down in her notebook to use later. She'd put on the Police, their last album, and pulled a blanket over her knees, trying to make a comfortable shelter from the tight space, fighting off fear. And why shouldn't she? Isn't this what it should look like, three sisters driving along the river at the end of summer? Singing "King of Pain" at the top of their lungs, the windows rolled down, the car swerving into the left lane in the high winds.

They reached Baie-Sainte-Catherine late in the afternoon, stopping in front of Le Vacancier, a row of blue-and-white cabins sandwiched between the road and the river. I can picture it clearly, how they pulled up near the restaurant and got out into the motel parking lot, their excitement as they hurried into reception to see about a room. It was their first time at a motel. But I no longer remember what they did after they brought their luggage to their room, whether the urn stayed in the trunk that night. The morning I remember though, because I wrote it all down in a little grey notebook: they went to sit by the water to watch the sunrise at the mouth of the fjord. Then they got back on the 138 until the road ended at the Saguenay River. It was maybe noon.

We hiked the Pointe-de-l'Islet trail, with the urn in my bag. I waited until we finished the first loop to take out the chisel I'd borrowed from my roommate in Montreal. My sisters stared at me, incredulous. I'd remembered the urn to be like a can of paint you open by sliding the blade of a knife under the lid for leverage—and I thought I was being clever, when Christelle had asked me to bring a screwdriver, to borrow the chisel, the end of which would easily squeeze between the lid and the box.

It had not for a second occurred to me that the box would be sealed shut with four small Phillips screws. I suggested we turn back and try to find a screwdriver in town. We set our sights on the first place we passed: Le Gibard, a pub with wood-panelled walls and a pink facade, a haven for touring artists and fishers after a day at sea. We had to hand the box over to the customers, and it went from one set of hands to the next until someone said he thought he had the right size screwdriver in the trunk of his car. I thought of Papa, how he'd probably have been the one to help us if he were here. The fishermen joked with us: once they got the box open we'd have to show them what was inside. We made no promises, just let them have at it.

It took a few tries. The screws were in tight. The box got passed around again, pausing on the counter. One screw came out, then another. The room was on edge, maybe because we were three women in a bar full of men, but mainly because of this strange box that would at any moment reveal its secrets. All three of us watched the box that held our father.

The last screw popped out, and one of us held out a hand, as calmly and naturally as anything, to rest it on the lid. The men protested. For a few seconds, I wondered what they'd say if we told them the truth. But we looked at each other, and we pulled the urn close. We walked out, a hand on the lid, saying thank you, thank you, everyone. I like to think a legend was born that evening in Gibard—because that's what fishers do, they invent stories from the bits of life that get away. A legend about three sisters and a mysterious box.

In the car, on the way back, I told myself the story: the fishermen had gone back to talking after the girls left, when they heard the metallic clamour of masts in the port. They went outside and, through the fog, saw a wave higher than anything they'd ever seen. It ripped up the docks, toppled the boats, snapped the masts in two, then receded back into the water. No one ever saw the three sisters again. But since that day, villagers tell the story of a man of around fifty, wandering the beach and calling his daughters' names, a man who never says a word to anyone.

At Pointe-de-l'Islet, we went off from the path to climb a rock overhanging the river. The urn was a rectangular box of blond wood, the lid held in place by screws, which we'd put back but hadn't tightened. Now I took them out. Everything was preserved in this box, everything you'd managed to do or say, everything you'd felt, the timbre of your voice, the marks on your skin, your smell, your childhood. In the movies, the urn is emptied into the ocean and a cloud of ashes scatters. But in the movies, the wind off the water doesn't sweep the ashes toward the shore in a thick cloud as the grains of burnt dead body gather in the hems of clothing, sting eyes and settle into hair like sand after a day at the beach. I didn't mind. I found it beautiful, and funny, to know it was you clinging in clumps to my lashes. I may have even opened my mouth a little, but I kept it a secret.

We sat on a rock and talked about you. The way we talked had changed. It was no longer about a father who used to fry up potatoes on Sundays, who drank more than he should have, who loved animals so much and his wife so poorly. We spoke of a father who no longer had a voice, a house or a body.

The cold cut short our conversation. The day was fading. I got up and looked at the water, rubbed my eyes to clear out the last specks of you. I liked to imagine we threw the urn in the water and it has been slowly decomposing at the bottom of the Saint Lawrence ever since. But I think we threw it in the trash on the drive back. It doesn't matter; you were no longer in it.

We did the trip home in reverse: the ferry, the motel, Baie-Saint-Paul, Quebec City. We left the river behind and re-entered the current of our lives, myself in Montreal, my sisters in Paris. I don't think of your ashes very often, only when I'm by the river in the summer and I dig my hands into the sand to make castles. Fragments of shell, rock and decomposed, burnt body collect under my nails. I clean out the small space between the nail and skin with a toothpick to keep up appearances. Your name is disappearing. The stories are what we have left.

People ask why we emptied your ashes into the Saint Lawrence. I think it was exactly this: to have a nice story to tell about you. The story of three sisters getting into a car with an urn to go scatter your ashes in the Saint Lawrence, a place you'd always dreamed of going. It's a nice story, it's true. And I owe it to them—to Christelle and Élodie, my sisters, your daughters. I couldn't appreciate it at the time, sick with grief as I was. But today I'm infinitely grateful that they delivered this madness to me, *"the pure insanity of a person contained in a tiny receptacle,"* for having insisted and braved my apparent indifference so we could have a nice story to tell instead of all the awful ones people struggle with when a father dies without warning.

Papa is dead. I often repeat that sentence to myself. I try to convince myself that the use of the verb *to be* prevents him from disappearing altogether.

Thirst

Outside, a light snow showers down. I want to open my mouth to catch the snowflakes and feel them melt on my tongue. I'm always thirsty, no matter how much I drink. I even wake in the night for water. My thirst is sated only when I'm drunk. And that happens less and less, given my weak liver.

I wonder if I've inherited this thirst from my father. Maybe alcoholism is imprinted in my genetic code, passed down from father to son before it reached me, of which only this unquenchable thirst remains, and which I stave off with litres of water. Maybe my father wasn't all that sad; maybe he was just thirsty.

/

The child is three, maybe four years old. Blond hair, square face. A black coat and bare legs. Behind him, crouching down, a young man puts his arms around him to help pull the string of a large bow into shooting position.

The Photo

My father is the kid. He's looking down at his brother's hands, which are holding the arrow perpendicular to the bow. Their shadows stretch across the cement yard, up to the stone wall. Half a woman's shadow leans into the frame—short curly hair, a flowing dress, maybe a bathrobe, arms crossed at her belly: their mother.

The photograph of my father with his brother is the only image we had seen of him as a child. My sister has the photo, and she keeps it in a frame on a shelf in her bedroom. It's a yellowed square, the corners damaged. I've often stopped in front of it without considering this image in particular: I was always struck by the two other photographs in the same frame. In the other two, my father is in his twenties. I easily recognize the sneaky look of his thin silhouette, his twitching muscles.

My father is with friends, but he's the one who catches your eye, just as he did in real life. I can spend ages dissecting these photos, looking for what gives him his aura. The little blond boy huddled near his brother inspires nothing, doesn't stir up any emotions. That child, my father, evokes only the yellowed hue of old family albums. On the back, the main characters reveal their identities: two first names, the first letters of which time has worn away, noted in rounded cursive.

His Name

How long before a name disappears, before it's struck from the official and unofficial lists of the living? Before it stops being passed down? Sometimes I imagine that the last time my father spoke his name aloud was to a government employee at the passport office. *How do you write that?* He answered that he couldn't write, except his name, which he spelled out. He added, *There used to be an accent on the a but they took it off. It was complicated enough.* And she asked, *Where's it from?* And he said, *State care.* The woman didn't look up. *First name?* she said. *Mario. Mario Édouard.* She raised her head, *Mario Édouard? Really?* His brother's name was Gaëtan. *Mario and Gaëtan, do you remember that show?* She shook her head.

My father never wrote a word: not a letter, not a note left on the table before going to work. Even on the postcards my parents sent us, my father's presence was always expressed in a little sentence—*a big hug from Papa*—in my mother's writing.

She was also the one who signed our homework, our report cards and notes sent home from school. If, for one reason or another, we asked our father to do it, he'd say he wanted to sign a cross, an X, like illiterates used to do. He wasn't illiterate, but he reiterated his rudimentary knowledge of the written language. It seems to me like a question of loyalty: he had the firm intention of having spent his life as part of a class of people whose names are forgotten. It was in solidarity with them. For me, the X looked like what pirates drew on their maps to mark the treasure.

He didn't have time to use his passport, and the box for his signature remained as empty as the pages that were supposed to be filled with stamps from the countries he would have visited. My mother took back her maiden name. My little sister has just taken her husband's name. And I in turn run from this name that my father passed down.

I never give it when I'm introduced. I hold out my hand, and I say, "Céline." That's it. But I'm well aware that one day, when no one says his name anymore, my father will finally have disappeared completely.

Scene 16

CHRISTELLE, CÉLINE, ÉLODIE

CHRISTELLE: I think he suffered a lot those last few months. I felt bad that I didn't see it. *(She pauses for a minute.)* But at the same time, it wasn't my job to know.

CÉLINE: Do you feel up to telling me about it?

CHRISTELLE: Yes, for sure. Where do you want me to start?

CÉLINE: *(Asking Élodie a question she's added to the transcription)* What caused his death?

ÉLODIE: I drew a blank when I read the text over. After all this time, that's not what's stayed with me. What caused his death? I think his whole body was giving out. Not much could be done by that point.

CÉLINE: Do you think he knew he was going to die?

ÉLODIE: I think he figured as much, yeah.

CÉLINE: *(To Christelle)* You can start with when you realized…

CHRISTELLE: He'd been sick since January. His family doctor said it was a virus. But it kept dragging on and on. I asked him to go back, but…you know how much he hates doctors. In April, he suddenly started losing weight, and he had no energy. That's when I started to worry, and I took charge. We had a first appointment in May. I was nervous. I thought they'd say Papa was too weak and had to be hospitalized. But they just gave him requisitions for some tests and sent him home. That felt like a good sign. He went back to the hospital for the tests. He was supposed to be out that same day, but the anesthesiologist wanted to keep him there. Because…well, because he didn't think Papa was in any shape to go home. That was Tuesday, and he stayed there the rest of the week. I went to see him on Friday. In the bathroom, there was a pile of clothes covered in blood. He was tired, and in a lot of pain, it seemed. I went to find the nurse. I wanted to know what was going on. "Has the doctor seen him? What's the treatment protocol? What happens next?" "My dad's not the kind to complain," I told them, "so you need to check on him once in a while to see if he needs anything." It was the receptionist who finally told me that the doctor was only in on Tuesdays, for consultations. He hadn't seen Papa since his tests; he hadn't even called to follow up or gone over treatment options. As far as he was concerned, Papa had gone home and everything was fine. The only thing the nurses were doing was giving him blood, because he was losing so much of it. When I saw that no one was looking after him, I kind of lost it. I told the receptionist she needed to do something. She managed to get a hold of the anesthesiologist, who took care of the transfer: Papa arrived at the hospital in Poissy that night.

Christelle asks Céline if she wants some tea. She fills two cups, takes a few sips.

CHRISTELLE: In Poissy, they did surgery during the night because… because his tumour was bleeding… They had to do something. And after that he went to intensive care. So I guess it's lucky that… *(She stops herself.)* If I hadn't said anything, I think they would have just left him to die that way. Slowly.

CÉLINE: That's when they put him in a coma?

CHRISTELLE: That's when they put him in a medically induced coma, yeah. So he wouldn't be in so much pain. He must have been in a pretty bad way the days before. *(Silence)* We went in on the Sunday, me and Élodie. No one had told us he was unconscious, they told us *(inaudible).* We got there with little cakes—you know, like you'd bring when you visit someone who's just had surgery—and when we got there, they looked at the cakes, and they said, "Oh…I guess no one told you." So the resident explained that it was pretty serious, that…that they had no idea how long he'd last, but they weren't optimistic. It was two weeks, from the time he saw the specialist for that appointment and his death. We didn't see it coming. None of us. The last time I saw him awake was the Friday when— *(She interrupts herself.)* He couldn't stand having to stay at that first place, even for those couple days. He realized it was probably serious…

Tears swallow up the rest of the sentence. Céline hands her a tissue and says something stupid—"That passage makes me cry when I read it too"—as if she were talking about a movie she'd watched often. Christelle smiles, tactfully, and keeps going.

CHRISTELLE: He realized it was probably serious because he said, casually, "Well, I guess I'll be at the hospital for the summer." So he knew he wasn't doing well, and I think he'd known for a long time. He just didn't want to… *(Her voice lowers.)* He didn't want to know. So that's it. That's how it happened: really quickly.

CÉLINE: *(Frowning as she reads)* I don't understand why no one told me sooner. Why you'd keep me in the dark.

She would like to erase this sentence from the transcription and from their minds—these traces of resentment that now seem uncalled for. Christelle reads the sentence gently while, three years ago, she'd read the words harshly.

CHRISTELLE: Except I didn't keep you in the dark. We found out that he was really sick on the Sunday, and I called you on Sunday. We didn't tell Mom because she was on vacation. Before Sunday, I thought Papa was just going in for a few tests. That's what the doctor had said: "We'll do a few tests." You don't call someone about a few tests. Just like I wouldn't have called you to say Papa was getting a tooth pulled. Because that's all it was. That's all.

CÉLINE: You didn't think it could be cancer?

CHRISTELLE: I didn't know if I… Yes, I did wonder, because I looked up his symptoms online. And I asked a doctor friend what she thought. She reassured me, "It's not always cancer. Don't worry too much." He hadn't been eating much; that could have explained the weight loss. And even after I found out it was cirrhosis, I never imagined he'd die that same week. But in the end, he had a tumour that was bleeding. Losing blood made the cirrhosis worse, and the cirrhosis stopped the blood from clotting. So the two conditions aggravated each other. But we didn't know any of that. We didn't ever exclude you from anything on purpose.

CÉLINE: When I found out he was having tests done, I spent the whole week wondering if I should fly home. I was worried it was serious; but there was also the chance I'd fly back for nothing, that I'd buy a ticket for nothing, when I was flat broke.

CHRISTELLE: That makes sense. It was complicated on our end too. Élodie will tell you the same. We didn't get to say a proper goodbye. I wish my last conversation with Papa hadn't been the one we had in the hospital. I have no clue what kinds of dumb things I said because I saw him in distress and I... I'll just say that the last few years with him weren't easy. He treated me like I was his mother, or his wife. I was the one who had to check every cupboard when I went to visit, to be sure there wasn't liquor in the house.

CÉLINE: Were you mad at him?

CHRISTELLE: No. I was worried. And scared. I cried all the time. I was... *(She says something inaudible.)*

ÉLODIE: *(To Céline)* Christelle arrived in Plaisir in a taxi. She broke the news to me. And then we went to the airport to get you. Then—do you remember? We used the money that was in Papa's wallet to have a picnic by the water.

CÉLINE: It was Christelle's idea. A sort of homage. He would have liked us to use the money that way, all of us eating cheese and salami together.

ÉLODIE: I had my yearly appointment at Bichat Hospital.

She smiles as she reads this sentence again.

CÉLINE: Why the smile?

ÉLODIE: Because there are all these minor details I still remember so clearly. I told the nurse, "I've just lost my dad, there's no point in me being here."

CÉLINE: I don't remember where we waited for you.

ÉLODIE: You went to the hospital in Poissy and back. Now, whenever I pass that hospital when we go to Mom's, I think of Papa.

CÉLINE: I don't think I've driven past it since. I wouldn't recognize the hospital anyway. I don't remember any of those details. Nothing that was happening made any sense. I was in shock.

ÉLODIE: We were all in shock. *(She explains what Céline doesn't seem to hear.)* I knew that sometimes Papa would get these heavy bleeds. But I didn't know how serious it was. When we brought him to the first hospital for those tests... *(She stops to correct the text.)* He needed to hold on to my arm to be able to walk. *(She adds the sentence at the end.)* It was such a strange feeling.

Scene 17

PHILIPPE, CÉLINE, CHRISTELLE,
MARC, ÉLODIE

PHILIPPE: I went over to visit a lot. Every two or three days. I could tell he wasn't doing good.

CÉLINE: He'd already stopped working at the farm by then?

CHRISTELLE: He'd found some work for a landscaper but didn't last long.

CÉLINE: Do you remember why he got fired from the farm?

CHRISTELLE: It was when Armelle took over the farm for her parents. Things had already been different. Papa would complain about the new methods; she'd studied agronomy and wanted to industrialize how they worked. It threw him.

CÉLINE: I think his pride was hurt too. He'd watched Armelle grow up. Having her tell him what to do without ever asking for his input, that just wasn't going to fly.

CHRISTELLE: They argued a lot. He could actually be kind of aggressive with her. But I think she fired him because...of the drinking.

CÉLINE: That was the official reason?

CHRISTELLE: Officially I think it was a layoff. But the drinking was a problem. He'd drive the farm trucks, even though he didn't have a licence anymore. And he worked with chemicals and tools. It was dangerous.

CÉLINE: He took it hard, losing his job?

CHRISTELLE: Definitely. It was all a huge blow, and he didn't have it in him to get back on his feet.

PHILIPPE: I told him he could come work with me and we'd split things fifty-fifty. I needed a hand, and your dad was good at everything. He came the first day, then didn't show up the next. I went by and rang the bell: no answer. Then I didn't see him for a stretch. When I finally ran into him, he told me he'd been sick.

"You doing better?"

"Yeah, much."

I told him I'd still give him half the cash for the contract. He needed the money.

"Forget it."

I offered him plenty of other contracts, but he'd never show up. I gave him shit. He didn't do anything anymore. Didn't fish. Didn't even own a fishing rod anymore.

CHRISTELLE: I think he was starting to get sick.

PHILIPPE: One time he told me he'd bought a brand-new fishing rod. He invited me fishing, then bailed. He claimed it was because of the dog. "You've got a BMW. My dog's going to scratch up the seats and mess up your car." That was bullshit. He always put the dog at his feet. *(He raises his voice.)* Did I give a shit if the mutt scratched my seats? Same thing when we had plans to go pick mushrooms. I swung by to pick him up so we could go morel picking, and he didn't come to the door.

218

CÉLINE: He was out?

PHILIPPE: He didn't always answer when I went by. I knew he was home. His scooter was in the yard, but he wouldn't come to the door. Other times he'd yell, "Give me five minutes." I think he was hiding bottles. After, I figured he was sick and didn't want me to know. *(Pause)* It was hard to tell what was true with him.

CÉLINE: Because he lied?

PHILIPPE: Constantly. Sometimes he pretended he couldn't go out with me because he was waiting for Élodie, but I'd call her and she'd say she hadn't planned on coming by. He told me a story about how he'd gone to the dentist to get his two rotted-out front teeth pulled. That wasn't true either.

CÉLINE: *(To Marc)* Did you realize he was sick?

MARC: When I ran into him, I could tell. *(He lets a long silence go by.)* But I didn't see him much anymore.

CÉLINE: Did seeing him feel awkward? Because of the separation?

MARC: I just didn't have time. It happened so fast. His old man hit the bottle hard his whole life, and he was fine. Your dad…

CÉLINE: I've often wondered if the farm work didn't have something to do with it. Maybe it had more to do with all the pesticides he'd been breathing in for twenty years and less to do with the drinking.

Christelle's eyes go wide when she reads this passage, and she looks up at Céline.

CHRISTELLE: I never thought of that.

CÉLINE: I talked to you about it in the first interview though.

CHRISTELLE: Maybe you did. *(She thinks about it.)* I don't remember anymore.

Céline remembers very well how Christelle had brushed it aside with a great deal of certainty the last time. "It's the drinking that killed him. There's never a single reason you get cancer. But for Papa, it's eighty per cent certain it was the drinking."

CÉLINE: People weren't talking about the effects of pesticides yet; we were aware of them, but we didn't talk about it. When we lived on the farm, on days when they'd spray the fields, Mom would close all the windows and tell us to stay inside. But Papa didn't take any precautions whatsoever when he worked: no mask, no gloves—ever.

CHRISTELLE: The day after they sprayed, we'd go out again and play hide-and-seek in the cornfields. *(They both laugh.)* It's true that everyone who worked on the farm died of cancer. *(She tilts her head to one side, then the other.)* At the same time, Gaëtan hadn't worked there long when he was diagnosed...and Hervé was really old when he died.

Céline insists, because she'd like to forget the man who drinks. It's such a powerful image that it erases all others. Sometimes, when people ask her how her father died, she says cancer. Just that. She's well aware of what the word cirrhosis brings to mind: the caricature, staggering, singing at the top of their lungs, the drunk who starts a brawl.

ÉLODIE: When we cleared out the apartment, we found a bag full of hard alcohol. *(Pause)* He deliberately sped things up.

CÉLINE: You mean…at the hospital? That he asked the doctor to speed things up?

ÉLODIE: No, no, before—with the drinking.

CHRISTELLE: At least, I tell myself, it's for the best that he went so fast.

CÉLINE: Why?

CHRISTELLE: He hated being sick. He hated hospitals.

/

Who's next on the list?

Scene 18

THE MOTHER, CÉLINE, ÉLODIE,
PHILIPPE, CHRISTELLE

THE MOTHER: I'm surprised Marc only talked about the trouble they got up to: getting arrested, stealing...

The interview with Marc is the only one that took place in front of a third party. It occurred in the presence of the mother, at her house.

CÉLINE: You'd been expecting him to talk about something else?

THE MOTHER: About their friendship. And about when things were bad between your father and me. About the end. *(She sighs.)* Maybe I shouldn't have been there.

CÉLINE: *(Gently)* Maybe. But it might also have been good for him to talk in front of you. You two didn't talk about Papa that often, I'm guessing?

THE MOTHER: Never.

CÉLINE: It's strange I never found your wedding photos.

THE MOTHER: All the photos I have of him are here. And Christelle has the rest.

CÉLINE: No, I asked her, and she said you have them.

THE MOTHER: Maybe they got thrown out. I know he put up pictures of you three on his bedroom door. Maybe they smelled like smoke and your sisters threw them out?

ÉLODIE: The neighbour's the one who cleaned the apartment after he died. She scrubbed the floors for hours…

CÉLINE: Cleaning out the apartment was difficult for me. It was all dealt with so quickly. I felt like we were hurrying to get rid of all his things so we could forget him as soon as we could.

ÉLODIE: That's the way you saw it?

CÉLINE: Yes. He never wanted to throw anything away. So it felt like a betrayal to empty his apartment so quickly.

ÉLODIE: *(Skipping over the first sentence)* There was no room. It's a shame, but things being what they were, well… *(She adds a sentence to what is written.)* Also, every object is a trace and, therefore, potentially painful.

CÉLINE: I think that's exactly what I miss about those objects we threw away: the memories that go with them. I'm not even sure, actually, whether we threw them away or gave them away.

ÉLODIE: *(Picking up the text where she left off)* Papa's collection of beer glasses, we gave that to Philippe. We figured he'd be happy to have it, since they were such old friends. But Philippe was broke and ended up having to sell it.

PHILIPPE: I took the beer glasses. Because your sisters said it's what your dad would have wanted. Personally, I don't like hanging on to stuff. It's too much of a reminder. I try not to stir all that up. What about the dog? Where'd he end up?

CÉLINE: I thought you were the one who—

PHILIPPE: I wanted to adopt it. But my dog was jealous. Didn't work out.

Earlier, he had said he'd have liked to keep it, but the neighbours had taken it. He even told me he went by to see how the dog was, but no one was home. He'd tried to find out more from the "gypsies across the street," but they didn't know anything about it.

ÉLODIE: The silver coins used to belong to Patrice; I got those. And then I took that small pipe you gave him, and his ID card. And I think you got his Laguiole, a pipe and his passport. Christelle took one of the other knives. I don't think we kept much else. *(She comments on the transcription.)* And I'm glad to have his signet ring somewhere. It's the only jewellery of Papa's left.

Céline had completely forgotten about his rings.

CÉLINE: Do you have his wedding ring too?

ÉLODIE: Grandpa's and Papa's rings both disappeared at the hospital. We asked the staff about them, Christelle and I. They said Papa didn't have them when he came into the hospital. He'd have wanted Jeanne to have them.

CHRISTELLE: What's funny is that Papa never cared about how much things were worth—it was the sentimental value. Everything he kept, he kept because it came from somebody. The glasses and the coins he'd inherited when Patrice died. The stamps too, I think.

CÉLINE: And the knives?

CHRISTELLE: Marc gave him his first. He couldn't accept a knife as a present without giving a franc for it. There's some superstition that if someone gives you a knife without anything in exchange, it can sever the bonds of friendship.

CÉLINE: *(Looking up from the script)* I forgot about that.

CHRISTELLE: Really? If he lost one, it was the end of the world. He'd search the house for it, retrace his steps from work back home. In the evening, we couldn't eat until all three knives were on the table. He believed in all that stuff. The bread couldn't be upside-down...

CÉLINE: *(Imitating her father's voice)* Because "you can't earn your daily bread lying on your back."

CHRISTELLE: And he never left the house on Saturday the fourteenth. There'd been an accident on a Saturday the fourteenth. He wasn't afraid of Friday the thirteenth, but he figured the world would end the day after.

CÉLINE: *(Holding up a photo for Élodie to see)* I scanned the pictures in Annette's albums. There was a wedding photo. On the back it says, "October 11, 1975." Which means Mom was already a few weeks pregnant with Christelle. Maybe she didn't know yet. *(Her voice steadies.)* I looked for the wedding album everywhere and I can't find it. Mom thought Christelle had it, but no.

ÉLODIE: *(Breaking from the text)* I think Papa took the pictures after the divorce, so they must be in the box.

CÉLINE: The box?

ÉLODIE: When we cleared out the apartment, I put a few things in a box. It's in Mom's garage. I can't remember what's in it. Probably records. And the photo albums. I don't know what kind of shape they're in. I keep saying I'm going to make time to go through it, but...

Sometimes anger wells up inside Céline when she thinks of how little their father left behind. But she thinks of the weight of all he took with him: what he never managed to say, what he misunderstood or would have needed to hear. What to do with all of that now?

Scene 19

PHILIPPE, ÉLODIE, CHRISTELLE,
CÉLINE, THE MOTHER

PHILIPPE: Near the end, no one came to see him. Except your sisters. Once some neighbours told me he'd been drinking again. They'd seen him stumbling through the village. I repeated what they'd said to your dad. He told me that was garbage. "Ask my daughter. She was with me." I asked Élodie: it was true. She'd been with him and he hadn't been drinking.

Céline hadn't called often and didn't stay on the line for long, saying she was busy with work or she had somewhere to be.

ÉLODIE: It was hard to want to go over there. I never knew how it would go. Sometimes he was fine; other times…it was more compli-cated. Christelle and I started going over together. It was easier, the two of us. Christelle handled his papers, his letters. It gave us something to talk about. *(She lowers her voice as if to confide something.)* I found him hard to talk to too.

CHRISTELLE: Philippe was there… He'd go see Papa. They had started speaking again and they would see each other once in a while. They went fishing together a few times, I think. I remember Philippe couldn't come to the funeral because he had to be somewhere. I'm not sure where. But he was sad. He was there right up to the end.

PHILIPPE: When we'd go for a walk, he couldn't manage the stairs at the town hall. He wasn't steady on his legs anymore. Not because he'd been drinking; he couldn't handle the walk.

He says he'll keep bringing his truck on the road with the carnival for a few more years. He sells crêpes, tartiflettes, churros, sandwiches, sausages and tartines. He gets by. He lives in the South of France six months a year. He tells Céline his girlfriend wants to break things off; Céline doesn't know what to say.

CÉLINE: Do you find it hard to talk about Papa?

PHILIPPE: When my brother said Mario's girl wanted to talk to me, he told me, "Get ready." I don't talk about your dad. Ever. It's too tough. You've stirred up a lot of stuff, and it's tough.

CÉLINE: I know. I'm glad you agreed to talk to me. His sister didn't want to. She doesn't want to talk about him anymore. She's been through too much. She told me, "All that is in the past, forgotten."

Later, a long time after this conversation, Céline went to see a therapist who specialized in trauma, who explained, "It's too much for some people." And she told Céline the story of a patient who had committed suicide after speaking about a traumatic event he had repressed for decades. "Some people can live their whole lives with that 'too much' feeling, because they've learned to live with its ghost-like presence in their lives, and with the psychosomatic symptoms these repressed memories cause. Whereas living with the conscious memories of an event—they just can't do it."

PHILIPPE: We can't just bury everything and forget. It doesn't work that way.

CÉLINE: We can tell ourselves we've forgotten. Or pretend.

PHILIPPE: No. We can't pretend. *(He tosses his cigarette.)* I ran into Jeannot a while back. He was one of the guys way back when. I told him your dad died. Jesus, did he take it hard. I don't get it. No one told your dad's friends.

Céline had tried to cancel the weekend in Normandie that Christelle had organized with their dad a few weeks before her big departure for Quebec. She'd called her sister to say she couldn't do it. She couldn't spend the weekend with her dad, eat breakfast with him, sleep in the same room. It wasn't that she didn't love him; it was the silence. Her father's silence burned into her, so that after a few hours with him she had to leave, to cool down again. Christelle had insisted.

CHRISTELLE: In the months after his death, I kept dreaming that he had come back to life. It was horrible because I felt ambivalent, between the happiness of seeing him and anxiety at having to take care of him again. I would go back to being an afterthought, and he would become my whole life again. *(She adds in a pause.)* Those last months I was so tired, at the end of my rope, that sometimes I would think about how much easier it would be if he died.

CÉLINE: I kept constantly thinking about the card I'd sent him. When he got it, he called me and said he hadn't managed to read it until the end the first time. I took that as a good thing—I was clearing the air. But after he died, I regretted it. I kept wondering if I had...

CHRISTELLE: The card rattled him.

CÉLINE: He told you about it?

CHRISTELLE: *(Slight pause)* Did he tell me about it? I don't really remember. But I know that, yes, it rattled him. He felt...

CÉLINE: Like I was accusing him of something?

230

CHRISTELLE: I'm not sure if it was that… It was more… *(She hesitates.)* Maybe that you were accusing him of something—yeah.

Céline wonders for the first time about the impact these interviews will have on her, on her memory.

CHRISTELLE: All I remember is that he had a hard time reading it, and it hurt him a lot. *(She rests her hand over her heart.)* Maybe he didn't understand what you were really trying to say; maybe he misunderstood because there were things he felt guilty about. I know it made him…sad. I'm not sure why exactly, or what it was in the letter he found hurtful. Maybe it was the fact he couldn't talk to you about it in person? Or that he didn't have the right words to answer? I have no clue.

CÉLINE: I needed to put something on paper about how we weren't close anymore, to try to fix things.

CHRISTELLE: In his mind there was nothing to fix. Any distance between you was geographical. That's all. He was looking forward to you coming back from Montreal; he was looking forward to seeing you and talking to you. That's what came as a shock: that you thought there was something that needed fixing.

CÉLINE: But it had been that way since I was a teenager.

CHRISTELLE: Honestly, I think you were just as responsible as he was for the way things were between you. You were super hard on our parents when you were a teen. You have to remember: you rejected everything about them, and told them as much.

CÉLINE: *(Whispers)* But he was hard on me too.

CHRISTELLE: I'm not sure. I don't remember, really, what your relationship was like. But I know Papa was always proud of you. He talked about you all the time after you moved to Montreal.

THE MOTHER: He thought you were too much like him, and he was scared about how you would turn out.

CÉLINE: That's why he was hard on me?

THE MOTHER: Because you're both so strong-willed. He told me, "We've got to rein her in." "Let's not be too quick to label her," I told him, "let's wait and see." Yes, that's what he was afraid of: that you'd get into trouble like he used to.

Céline thinks about the card again, about the irrational fear she'd felt after his death. Even now, the only things she writes to family or friends are thoughtful notes and pleasantries.

CÉLINE: I kept thinking that I killed him with what I wrote. Or that it precipitated his death, that he died deliberately before I got there so he wouldn't have to see me.

CHRISTELLE: *(Firmly)* That's ridiculous. That's not what happened. I know your card rattled him. But that wasn't the reason things happened how they did. In the end, it was because he was sick, and because Papa had given up long before he got your card.

Céline has very few memories of that weekend in Normandy: a vague recollection of a village fair by the sea, and another of an unexpected moment of closeness between them in the room in the morning. She also has a photograph. Just one. Her father is wearing a lightweight white shirt, rolled up to the elbows, and a pair of jeans and sneakers. It's a profile shot, one leg stretched out, his foot resting on a rock in an explorer's stance. He's looking into the distance, a hand shielding his eyes from the sun. His hair is short. His beard is greying at the chin. There are tourists in the background, probably staring out at the sea or the cliffs, but the photo is framed around her father, not the view.

/

I like to think that maybe each of us was his favourite, in our own way.

Scene 20

ÉLODIE, CÉLINE, PHILIPPE

ÉLODIE: When I read my interview, it brought back a lot of memories. For instance, I'd completely forgotten about sledding at the farm. It all came back. Remember how our butts used to burn after? I could even feel it. *(They laugh.)* I was nervous about your project at first, because I was afraid it would bring up bad memories. But I feel like overall it was a good thing. I've realized all wounds scar over with time. The mark is still there. It never disappears completely. It's painful, but when we think of it, it's with acceptance. That's how we grew up; it's how we became who we are today.

CÉLINE: The conversations didn't really reconstruct Papa's life in the end, because of all the different memories and how they diverge. But they allowed multiple versions of the story to exist.

PHILIPPE: *(After a moment's hesitation)* There's one person who— He changed her life. Annick Tanne. They were together a long time. From fourteen to seventeen. He left her. Never said why. Not even to me. When I asked why he broke up with her, he said, "That's life." She was crazy in love with him. She never got over it.

Céline never found her, this Annick Tanne, despite putting ads in the local papers and posting online. Her name wasn't on record at the town hall of the village where Philippe said she lived. Later, the name didn't quite seem to fit. She tried to imagine different combinations. Annie Quetanne, Annie Khtan, Anne Hiketan... She never got a chance to ask Philippe for more information.

PHILIPPE: Hang on. There was someone else as well…but she goes by a different name now. She got married. She loved him a lot too.

They put on their coats, their shoes. They get ready to leave the mother's apartment, where the interview took place while she was out. Before they go, Céline takes a roll of aluminum foil from the kitchen cupboard, rips off a piece, shapes it in her hands and empties the ashtray of cigarette butts amassed during their conversation. Like she used to when she was a teenager, to erase all traces of her friends.

PHILIPPE: How's your mom doing?

CÉLINE: She's good. She met someone.

PHILIPPE: Ah.

For a few seconds, he stands silently in front of Céline.

PHILIPPE: What do you want to do with all this then? With what I've told you?

CÉLINE: I'm not really sure. I wasn't there, and I wanted to understand who he was. As a person.

PHILIPPE: He was a good guy, your dad. Always there when I needed him. He had a rough go. Losing his job messed him up. But even before that, he'd lost his… He'd lost enthusiasm for everything.

CÉLINE: He had talked about buying a camper van and heading down toward central France.

PHILIPPE: That'd be the dream. Not going to happen for me. I served three months for fraud, and I have to stay put. Couldn't do it with my bad leg anyway. What about you? How are things in Canada?

CÉLINE: Everything's good. I had a hard time when I first got there… It was a struggle. But things are fine now.

PHILIPPE: He talked about you a lot. He didn't like that country of yours. It pissed him off that you'd left. But sometimes he'd say, "She's living her life."

She'd like to know what else her father used to say about her and her new country, but she doesn't venture the question. Next time. Next time she'll ask.

PHILIPPE: He talked about your sisters a lot too. Boy, did he love those girls. He loved all of you! Christelle—I used to run into her in Paris sometimes.

They're in front of his truck now. Philippe points to the supermarket.

PHILIPPE: What did that place used to be called again?

CÉLINE: I'm not sure.

PHILIPPE: You could ask your dad for any record. He'd go steal it for you there.

CÉLINE: He never got caught?

PHILIPPE: Never.

Staring at the ground, Céline sweeps aside some pebbles with her shoe.

CÉLINE: Papa wanted to go to Canada. He wanted to visit me.

It slips out and she's not sure why. He doesn't answer.

PHILIPPE: You know, I checked in on him all the time because I was scared he'd do something stupid. He'd ask me a few times to get stuff for him.

CÉLINE: What stuff?

PHILIPPE: He knew I could get guns. He asked me to get him one. "What do you want with one of those?" He didn't want to say. I told him I'd look into it, but I never got him a piece. *(Pause)* He lost enthusiasm for everything. He didn't even want to go fishing or pick mushrooms anymore. *(Pause, then very slowly)* He never said anything. Near the end, I mean. The idiot never said he was sick. It was just, "I'll be fine." When I'd tell him he should get out of the house, he'd say he was fine where he was, alone. He had his TV and the animals. He said he couldn't go out, not with the cats. The cats and the dog. He never said anything. Just like Gaëtan. He was in pain, but he waited until the end to tell anyone.

Philippe asks Céline to look him up the next time she's in town, tells her again how she's like a daughter to him. On that note, they say goodbye. And right away, Céline wants to call her cousins to ask them to give their dad another chance. But she also thinks of the hurt she caused in the past when trying to speak her truth—a truth Céline has a harder time holding on to as time goes by.

Three years later, she'll ask her mother for Philippe's address to organize the second interview. Her mother will be surprised. "You didn't know? He died. Cancer. I must have forgotten to tell you."

INVENTORY OF THINGS THAT LEFT NO TRACE

List of the books I had wanted to read to my father.
List of dreams about my father I didn't write down.
List of things my father lost.
List of things he would have wanted to change.
List of things he didn't think needed saying.
List of meals he liked to eat.
List of names he would have chosen for me if I'd been a boy.

/

Jasper Motel, route 185.

/

...and yet there is hardly a word of truth
in what they have said.
—Plato, *Apology*

DISAPPEARANCE OF A NAME

The French word *haha* is an archaism designating a way with no exit, a cul-de-sac, a dead end, or unexpected obstacle.

—Geographical Names Board of Quebec, Saint-Louis-du-Ha! Ha!

I was the life of the party back then, you know. I say this to my daughter as she walks up the 185 next to me, and she answers, "I know, Papa, I know. You've told me a hundred ti—" and a huge semi-truck swallows the rest of her sentence.

I live on route 185, in room seven of the Jasper Motel, between Saint-Honoré-de-Témiscouata and Saint-Louis-du-Ha! Ha!, just under an hour from Rivière-du-Loup and a good thirty minutes on foot from Marta's grocery store. José, Marta's husband, is a good guy. When I'm broke he lets me pay for my beer with the firewood I split by the motel in exchange for a discount on the rent. And we both weather the winter this way, hang on without suffering too much. Often Marta adds a carton of fresh eggs to my basket and asks after the girls. She says she wants to move to Montreal to be closer to her son, who doesn't come up anymore since his baby was born, but José doesn't want to leave. She juts her chin a couple times in his direction, and José mutters and walks off. She turns back to me, sighs. "Here," she says, "take some eggs. For your daughter. Say hello to her for me."

Céline has just arrived. She got here in the dead of night, talking a mile a minute and still tense from driving on edge, watching for deer—a fear that kept her alert the whole drive. She dozed off not long before dawn, when the motel's red neon sign turned off and sounds started stirring in the adjoining rooms. I told her she should stay in bed while I went to get the bread and eggs at José's, but she said she was fine and the walk would give her legs a stretch. I smiled. The way to José's is a solid climb in full sun along the gravel strip that runs beside the road. Some July mornings the air is so sticky that I stop halfway and sit on the scorching earth for a smoke, and watch the humid air contort the landscape.

A truck passes, and the wind in his slipstream makes us jump to the side. Céline asks why I live eight kilometres from the nearest town when I don't have a car. Kind of dumb, no? I'd like to tell her all the reasons I chose this spot, but with all the cars going by, it's impossible to talk.

The night I arrived at the motel, room seven was the only one left. It's a big room with two double beds and a faded flower-print sofa facing a TV. As soon as I paid, the guy went out to add a *No* in front of *Vacancy* to the sign off the road. It was a warm night. No AC, so I pushed the comforter off the bed and turned on the fan. When I woke up the next morning, the parking lot was deserted.

I turn toward Céline, who's walking a metre behind me. Out of breath, her hands on her hips, she asks whether I brought any water. She was no more than three years old and her sister was five that day we walked from the house to the hospital, where their mother was giving birth to their little sister. It was late July, the heat so thick it levelled the houses on the horizon. I'd often taken the path through the fields alone—an hour, hour and a half if you dawdled. But with two kids it took the whole afternoon. Céline kept yelling because her shoes were too tight and she couldn't walk, and Christelle glared at me the whole way as I pulled on their arms to keep them moving. When we got to the hospital, my wife had already given birth and named the baby. The nurses put Christelle and Céline in a tub of cold water, horrified, scolding me, and then stuck them with a needle to hook up an IV to rehydrate them. My wife cried, little Élodie asleep on her chest.

No, I answer Céline. I didn't bring any water. It'll be okay. We're almost there. We'll pick up a bottle at José's. She shrugs, a truck passes close, and we bump into each other. She smiles. Sometimes I wonder why she still comes up to see me. I ask her. "Why do you still come to see me?" She throws up her hands dramatically, yells out something that another big rig swallows up. "Never mind," she says. "There's no point trying to talk." We see the sign for the store up ahead. I stop for a second and pull a handkerchief from my pocket to wipe my forehead. She watches me unfold it and wipe it across my face, then roll it into a ball and put it back in my pocket.

"We should have taken my car."

"Don't worry, it's downhill on the way back."

She keeps complaining. "It's not me I'm worried about, Papa."

"What exactly are you worried about?"

My question throws her off a little.

"Am I not allowed to worry about you?"

We walk into José's, and he looks up from the counter. "Hey, old man," he says.

I ask him what's new. Céline smiles shyly instead of saying hello, and heads toward the big fridges at the back. It's not going great: he and Marta had a fight yesterday and he had to drive her to the station in Rivière-du-Loup. Before she gets onto the bus to Montreal, she tells him she wasn't kidding this time, it's over. It's not the first time she's said it, but this time he feels like it's different. He always says that. Their son just called. He doesn't mind if Marta stays with him. She can help with the little one, the cleaning and all that.

"She'll be back. You'll see."

"I guess time will tell."

I don't know what else to add. At least this way, I tell him, she won't be riding his ass all the time. He says it's been dead around here since she left.

"And yourself?" he asks me.

"Same old. Not bad."

Actually, I'm already dead.

I had a life once—a wife, three daughters—and I drank and drank and drank. I thought I could forget myself. But I died before I could manage. When my wife left me, I was already dead. José glances over at my daughter and asks what he can get us. "We'll take some bacon, some eggs. A bag of potatoes. Six non-alcoholic beers." He goes over to the fridge at the back to fill my order, and I shout after him, "And a cider." Céline looks at me. She's carrying two bottles of water, a basket of strawberries balanced on them, a bag of chips at the top of the tower.

"We should've brought my car."

"Quit your complaining and give me those."

"You don't have any money, Papa. Let me pay."

José comes back with two full bags, puts them on the counter.

"And a 6/49? Céline will pick the numbers."

Instead of saying thank you, Céline laments, "You never change," and gives José heck. "You shouldn't let him buy those damn things."

José doesn't answer. I tell him to put it on my tab, and I grab the bags, one in each hand, and go outside to light a cigarette and wait for Céline.

The guy staring back at me in the storefront window has changed a lot, contrary to what Céline thinks. His hair, thin and greying, has receded to the middle of his skull, the shorn memory of a good chunk of his life. The hand holding the cigarette is wrinkled and streaked with blue lines, and his fingertips are yellow from nicotine. Everything in my past, all the shit I've lived through in the last forty years, has blurred together, muddled, like I'm coming out of anesthesia. I wear traces of it on me: heavy, puffy eyelids, hands that shake when I get up in the morning, the painful feeling that life is going too quickly. I wish I could escape what's keeping me here—the comforter, the brown curtains I draw every night to hide the stretch of the 185 and the cars racing down it day and night, as though they had nowhere left to stay. The one time Céline tried to talk to me about it, I told her not to bother. I don't know. I guess I was just afraid of what she wanted to settle with me.

Céline pushes open the door and waves a lottery ticket at me. "Here—your winning ticket." I don't tell her that with my luck my numbers will come up this week, the one time I don't play them, even though I've never missed a draw. The store door closes behind Céline. She picks up a bag and starts walking down the hill. A few minutes and several cars later, she says, "José's funny. He asked me what your name was. He seemed embarrassed about it."

"What'd you say?"

"The truth—that we don't remember anymore."

I stop and look at her. "So you've forgotten too?"

She lowers her head, seems to search deep. "Yes, me too."

And she keeps walking, looking straight ahead. We keep going in single file, her in front, passing her bag from one arm to the other because it's too heavy. I don't offer to take it. She wouldn't let me anyway. I ask if she wants to go swim in the lake this afternoon. She didn't bring a bathing suit. She can go in her underwear, I say, who cares? I can almost hear the face she makes. We'll see, she says. A few cars pass us. "The Davids might come too. With their kids." She asks if the Davids are the ones with the white cottage on the 232, just outside Saint-Louis. I say, yes, the white cottage, that's the one.

The girls didn't inherit the house their mother and I had paid a mortgage on every month for more than twenty years. We had barely been able to pay the bank back with the money from selling the house, and when I died the taxes took half of what was left. The day of the cremation, they decorated the church with sunflowers like the ones we used to bring back from our walks when the girls were small. We'd cut the heads off and let them dry out in the sun, to harvest the seeds. The sunflowers in the church were supposed to help keep me there a bit longer, I think, but my body disappeared in the end. And death took more than my body; it took chunks out of the years I'd lived until nothing was left but the vague story of a man who drank, whose name no one remembers anymore. But all they have to do is ask, and I'd tell them my name. I'd tell the story of my life, pieced together in random memories as they come up, out of order.

In the meantime, I watch my daughter walking ahead of me. She's telling me she doesn't know whether she'll leave this afternoon or tomorrow morning, to avoid traffic. I understand. One time, she told me that if I'd died in some gruesome accident, she'd maybe have regretted never having a real conversation with me. "Very funny," I said.

We reach the yard in front of the motel. I point out the cat stretched in the sun in front of my door. I pick up a rock and throw it in the cat's direction. It stops grooming itself, lifts an ear and keeps licking, as if to say, *All right, show's over.* Céline turns to me and huffs, "What's your problem? What did you do that for?" I tell her I didn't hit the cat, and anyways, she knows it was just a joke. She drops her bag at my feet and pushes into the room first.

When they were little, the girls had a striped cat that slept with them. I wonder if Céline remembers. The cat got scabies and I was afraid the kids would catch it. I brought it out behind the house, tied it to the fence, took a step back and shot it with my rifle. Then I rolled the body in a blanket and buried it far back from the house, on the other side of the dirt road, so the girls wouldn't see. I couldn't come back until the evening. I reeked of booze. We told the girls the cat found a girlfriend and they went off on a trip together.

I go inside the room. Céline is in the bathroom. I put away the groceries. The first few months, I got by with just a cooler. I refilled it every two days with a bag of ice. But in the end I installed a small fridge, which I managed to squeeze between the wall and the dresser the TV sits on. To reach inside the fridge, you need to crouch behind the flowered sofa. A few months back, I bought a camping stove. When I'm alone, I eat at the motel restaurant and the small stove stays in its box until Céline's next visit. I barely even have coffee in the mornings these days. Next to the TV, the coffee machine is gathering dust on a flowered tray, the complimentary paper filter and packet of coffee still intact. The cleaner doesn't come every day anymore.

"Céline, is an omelette okay?" I ask through the bathroom door. I boil water on the burner that I pull out of the cupboard and I start thinking about what I need to say to her. I'm going to tell her I'm almost there, that I haven't touched those bottles under the bathroom sink in a week.

I pour boiling water into the mugs, add a spoonful of instant coffee and stir, put down the pot, put the frying pan on the gas, throw in bacon and beaten eggs and wait five minutes to call out that it's ready. Céline pushes open the door, a towel wrapped around her wet hair. I hand her the plate. "Thanks, Papa," she says, "it smells good." She sits on the edge of the bed she slept on last night and balances the plate on her thigh. I tell her that if she stays tonight, we'll eat at the motel restaurant and build a fire in the yard. She nods.

CARD FROM A FATHER TO HIS DAUGHTER

On the postcard, we see people facing away, looking at an almost-green sea. The beach is tiny, bordered by limestone cliffs, grooves worn in by the water. Below the photo is a drawing of a small smiling sun and the name of the region: Algarve. The postmark has been partly erased. The time it was sent can be made out, but not the date. I found this card inside a second-hand book I bought in Montreal the year I arrived.

Albufeira, April 14
My dearest daughter,

There are cactuses all along the path down to the ocean!
I couldn't help but think of you.
It's all too much to take in at once, it's like a dream.
Sending you a big hug.
Tell anyone who will listen that Portugal is the most beautiful country on earth.

Love, dad

So this is how they live on, the objects belonging to our dead—
heartbreaking and stupid.

—Marie Darrieussecq, *Being Here Is Everything*
(tr. Penny Hueston)

A Note on the Text

In the section "Or Even Dead Already," the author has woven quotes into the text by Christian Boltanski, Charles Pennequin, Thierry Hentsch, Romain Gary, the *Dictionnaire en ligne des règles orthographiques et de grammaire*, Catherine Mavrikakis, Nicolas Lévesque, Leonardo da Vinci, Thomas Bernhard (tr. David McLintock), Raymond Carver and Gwenaëlle Aubry (tr. Trista Selous).

All quotations in the book from works in French without an existing translation are the translator's own translations.

The photographs and other documents are from the author's personal archives and the flea market.

Acknowledgements

I would like to thank the members of my family and friends of my father who agreed to delve back into the past despite how painful it was.

Thank you to Guillaume Bellon, Nicholas Fizzano, Gwendolina Genest, Hubert Hayaud, Pascaline Knight, Pierre-Louis Malfatto, Jacques Perron, Karen Trask, Gabrielle V. and Ingrid Vallus for filling out a questionnaire about someone they only knew through me.

Thank you to Sylvie Chermet-Carroy for the handwriting analysis of my father's signature.

In its first incarnation, *Remnants* was a self-published art book printed in 100 copies in 2017. Thank you to Pier-Philippe Rioux and Catherine Métayer for their work designing and editing this first version. Thank you to my editor, Alexie Morin, who saw the potential for it to become a literary work at Le Quartanier, where the French-language version was published. Thank you to Aleshia Jensen, who penned this magnificent translation, and to Jay and Hazel Millar for letting it find a home at Book*hug and letting it to continue its journey in English.

I would not have been able to finish the book without the time and space provided by artist residencies at Passa Porta in Brussels, Atelier Circulaire in Montreal, and without the support of the Conseil des arts et des lettres du Québec and the Canada Council for the Arts.

Lastly, thank you to my friends and my fellow artists and writers. Especially to N.F. and S.P., whose real-life and imagined conversations nourished my writing.

To my sisters, Christelle and Élodie, and my mother

About the Author

Céline Huyghebaert is an artist and a writer. Her work, at the intersection of visual arts, language and literature, has been exhibited in France and Canada. In 2019, she won the Governor General's Award for her first novel, *Le drap blanc*, published by Le Quartanier, and she was awarded the Bronfman Fellowship in Contemporary Art. Born in France in 1978, she has been living in Montréal since 2002.

About the Translator

Aleshia Jensen is a French-to-English literary translator and former bookseller living in Tio'tia:ke/Montréal. Her translations include *Explosions* by Mathieu Poulin, a finalist for the 2018 Governor General's Literary Award for translation; *Prague* by Maude Veilleux, co-translated with Aimee Wall; as well as numerous graphic novels, including work by Julie Delporte, Catherine Ocelot, Mirion Malle, and Pascal Girard.

Colophon

Manufactured as the first English edition of
Remnants
in the spring of 2022 by Book*hug Press

Edited for the press by Katia Grubisic
Copy edited by Stuart Ross
Proofread by Rachel Gerry
Type + design by Tree Abraham

Printed in Canada

bookhugpress.ca